JOSIE

BY THE SAME AUTHOR

Books and stories:

BELLEEK – A CELEBRATION

A FIGHT FOR FREEDOM

THE FINAL KICK

Stage Plays:

THE CANDIDATE

THE WILL

WEDDED BLISS

Radio Play:

ON ACTIVE SERVICE

JOSIE

A STORY OF REVENGE

OLIVER MURPHY

First published in 2021 by Gullion Press

ISBN: 978-0-9931917-2-5

Cover design by Patrick Clarke
clatrickparke@gmail.com

gullionpress@gmail.com
@gullionpress
www.facebook.com/gullion.press

This novel is dedicated to my two dear brothers Finbarr and John who passed away shortly after each other, perhaps because neither could live in the other's absence. I dedicate it also to my sister Eilish who cared for them both with unstinting compassion, devotion, and love.

The axe forgets
the tree remembers

– African proverb

1

The patrol car swung into my front drive. Whirling lights created ghostly blue rainbows on pelting sheets of rain, reminding me of the Aurora Australis I had once witnessed on one of my previous attempts to escape the law, and maybe myself as well. No sirens blaring, just the noise of wheels crunching through granite gravel on the stately avenue, and a small skid when the car came to a halt at my front door. I stood at the window waiting and wondering: had these guardians of the law come too late . . . much too late?

The engine was killed, the windscreen wipers stopped slapping, and two gardaí emerged smartly. I opened my front door wide to greet them.

'Good morning,' I said.

One of them, a sergeant, donned his peaked cap and manoeuvred it around until it settled comfortably on his head.

'What's good about having to come out here in this damned rain?'

I stood in the open doorway. 'I've been to parts of the world where rain has more value than gold.'

'Yeah, well you're in Monaghan now.'

The sergeant stayed at the foot of the steps leading up to

the portico. 'Love is my name,' he said. 'This is Garda Fowler.'

'Stand in,' I said. The cops climbed the steps and huddled together like hens taking shelter in a storm. Fowler kept a respectful silence in the presence of his superior officer and gazed down the long tree-lined avenue, a scene that would only be complete with a splendid carriage and pair of white horses trotting along it.

I wondered how much they knew about the history of the place. Did they know about the IRA burning out the landlords in the twenties? Love would certainly have heard the stories.

'What's the situation?' said the sergeant. 'I should be at home watching *The Fugitive*.'

'I'm sorry to disrupt your plans, Sergeant.'

'Where is it?'

'In the big meadow.'

Love hunched his shoulders and buried his chin into his chest at the thought of going out in the rain. 'What were you doing out on such a day?' he asked.

'I've been checking the shores.'

'Oh yeah?'

'The drainage system is old.'

'Fowler, secure the car,' said the sergeant, before turning to me. 'I hope this isn't some kind of wild goose chase. I'm getting too old to be traipsing about muddy fields in a bloody monsoon.'

I didn't say anything. Fowler joined us, and I led the two policemen towards the meadow. All three of us kept our heads down against the driving rain. We passed the old sundial at the end of the garden. My father once told me that this type of clock was the only one that never needed winding. I remembered wondering how they knew the time at night. The deluge of water pelting us was even heavier when we walked under the line of old chestnut trees. After going through the first field, Love called out, 'How much further is it?' The peak of his cap resembled a leaking tap.

'Not far,' I said.

I couldn't make out his grunted response.

By the side of the big meadow, a human hand was sticking out of the ground. It had been washed clean of mud by the rain. Little veins resembling blue string worms were visible behind the knuckles. The fingers, a kind of ghostly white, were spread wide like a five-pronged fork. Faint traces of red varnish remained on once-manicured nails.

Fowler leaned over as if to touch it.

'Don't,' said the sergeant. 'You might be contaminating important evidence.'

I suspected that much of the evidence had been washed away. The rain ran down the side of the sergeant's face. Maybe he was thinking that the sun should be shining like it does at murder scenes in detective shows on television.

'What'll we do?' asked Fowler.

'Get me a stick,' said Love.

Fowler pulled a fallen branch from the nearby drain and gave it to him. We both watched as the sergeant knelt down on one knee like an old man at mass. He gingerly touched the tip of the thumb with the stick. After prodding it carefully for a few seconds, he said, 'Rigor mortis has set in.'

He cleared his throat and took a deep breath. 'I will now

commence to reveal more of the torso,' he said in a professional voice, the way a bomb disposal expert might describe every move to his comrades at a safe distance.

He edged away the soil from where the wrist protruded. More of the limb was revealed. Then a tiny bit more. This is going to take forever, I said to myself. Then the hand toppled over. Love fell backwards on his behind.

'God almighty,' said Fowler. 'It fell off.'

There was no sign of an arm or a body. Love got up and looked down at the hand for a few seconds. 'We'll have to cordon off the area and call in forensics.'

The hand now lay on its back. The skin on the palm was stretched tight like a drum. Fowler seemed rooted to where he stood.

In the squad car on the way into the police barracks there was little talk. Love wanted a statement of events from me. I kept thinking it would be short as there wasn't much I could say, except that I found the hand.

I asked him if there were any females reported missing.

He glanced back at me from the passenger seat. 'That information isn't for public consumption.'

His caginess seemed strange to me. He was more forthcoming when I enquired if he'd much experience handling murder cases.

'Oh yes, several violent deaths,' he said. 'The most recent just a month ago, a man shot in the back of his head. But those aren't real murders.'

'Why not?'

'They all had political ramifications.'

'I thought there was no IRA now,' I said.

Love said a united Ireland was still the dream of many, and there were always people prepared to resort to violence to achieve it. 'This county of ours has more IRA sleepers than there are bugs in a guesthouse mattress. Not surprising I suppose, considering our history.'

'You mean recent history?'

'Well, it's only a few years since one of our own sons of Monaghan was shot attacking an RUC barracks in the North, but even in the twenties the IRA was very strong in this area.'

I detected in the sergeant's voice a mixture of admiration and disdain, and decided his occupation as upholder of the law must have caused him mixed feelings.

When we got to the barracks, Love asked me to wait in the reception area while he prepared to take down my statement. I didn't know what preparations he needed. The place was a hive of activity with lots of officers coming and going, but all of them took time to stop and stare at me. I sat on a bench placed against the back wall, wondering how people had been able to scratch their names on it while in clear view of the garda at the reception desk.

The room, which badly needed painting, had various notices pinned to the wall, many of them relating to farming issues. One gave instructions on when to spray ragwort. Another warned that holding guns without a licence was a serious criminal offence. After listening to Love I wondered if the IRA would be daunted. A list of social services had their contact numbers stuck up. The first number was an Alcoholics Anonymous helpline.

Members of the public kept coming in to get various

documents signed or to make enquiries. There must be a factory somewhere in the world that manufactures these police reception areas. I had seen the inside of others and noticed very little difference in any of them. A sullen resentful atmosphere was always the predominant feature. Dinginess also appeared to be an essential characteristic. A middle-aged man in a suit and bright red tie sat down beside me. He said the court had ordered him to present himself every day at the barracks. I didn't ask the nature of the charges.

Eventually I got called into the sergeant's office. There was another person present who Love introduced as Detective Dooley. He was assessing me, and I him. I guessed he was in his thirties. His blond hair would have been unusual in Monaghan. He was holding a nail-file, and I looked at his hands. The nails were perfectly manicured.

'Ok,' said Love, briskly, 'let's get started. I want to begin by confirming a few facts concerning yourself. Some necessary preliminaries. You live alone, Mr Walker?'

I wasn't very happy about this approach. Surely I was there to make a statement, not to be questioned about my own circumstances, but I decided not to raise any objections. I figured he knew I lived alone, and felt like saying I had a mouse for company somewhere in the kitchen.

'Yes.'

'Are you not lonely?'

'No.'

'You're not afraid on your own?'

'No.'

'Maybe you're a brave man?'

'Brave as the next, I guess.'

'I have heard people say you're very wealthy.'

'People will say what they will say.'

The sergeant studied my face for a second, and then said, 'You were out checking the shores in the meadow when you found the body?'

'When I found the hand.'

'Ok, the hand, although I don't think it would be stretching the imagination to think that where you have a hand you will have an arm, and where you have an arm there is almost certainly a torso, i.e., a body. Wouldn't you say so, Detective Dooley?'

The detective squirmed a little in his chair. 'Mr Walker is of course correct to say he found a hand, but there is seldom a hand without a body.'

I could see the detective didn't want to make the sergeant look foolish.

'So you were checking the drainage when you found the hand,' said Love. 'Did you notice anything else unusual?'

'Such as?'

'I don't know. If I did I would mention it.'

'Would you say you have any enemies?' asked Dooley.

'The Crowleys weren't too happy with me buying the estate.'

'Ah, that's right,' said Love, leaning back in his chair with his hands joined across his chest, his eyes firmly fixed on me like some kind of smart detective in a movie. 'We all know about that.'

I held his eye, not wanting to let him intimidate me.

'Have you any idea who the deceased is?' I asked Dooley, who had been sitting with his elbow on the armrest of the chair, fiddling with the nail-file through the fingers of one hand.

'We're working on that.'

'I'm obviously not a detective, but I would have thought finding out the identity of the victim is the first priority.'

'The truth is,' said Love, 'we know very little about who *you* are. You turn up here in Cambroestown and buy McArdle's old mansion in the face of the Crowleys, who have been waiting on it coming to the market for years. We understand you spent much of your life in Australia. Other than that we know nothing about you.'

'I could say I know nothing about you except that you're the local garda sergeant.'

'It's said you have an interesting past.'

'We all have a past.'

Love leaned forward in his chair. 'Sometimes the past has a way of coming back to haunt you.'

'I have a past. You have a past. What's the difference?'

'The difference is human remains have been found on your land.'

'I reported finding the body.'

'Oh, so it's a body now,' said Love, pleased with himself. 'You're a stranger, Mr Walker, and you don't seem willing to disclose anything about yourself.'

'There isn't anything to disclose.'

Love gave his head a little nod, and said, 'Hmmm.'

'Do you suspect me of having something to do with the hand?'

'Don't jump the traces,' said Love. 'What we are saying is we don't believe Old McArdle went around burying women on his land.'

Dooley had resumed checking his nails, every so often giving one of them a little rub with the file. 'One of the first things we are taught in training is to take particular note of coincidences,' he said, holding one hand out in front of him with the fingers spread for inspection.

'And?' I said.

'A total stranger turns up in the quiet little hamlet of Cambroestown. He buys what was once the big house belonging to the old aristocracy. Shortly afterwards, human remains are discovered on the land.' He lowered his hand and stared at me. 'Surely those events could be classed as coincidences?'

Just then there was a little knock on the door. It opened and a head appeared. 'Sergeant, can I speak with you a moment?' said the newcomer.

Love left the room. Dooley idly resumed his manicuring. 'We don't have much serious crime here,' he said. 'It's mostly political stuff. You're not politically-minded I take it.'

'I have no interest in politics,' I said.

'Just what are your interests?' asked Dooley.

Before I could answer, Love came back into the room. He went over and whispered into Dooley's ear. I saw a look of surprise appear on the detective's face, then the sergeant turned to me and said, 'There's been a development.'

'Oh yeah?'

'Only the hand has been recovered. There's no sign of the rest of the body.'

'That's strange,' was all I could think to say.

'You appreciate it will mean extensive searching, extending to the big house,' said Dooley.

'Do I have any say in the matter?'

'In my experience,' said Love, 'it's always best to be cooperative.'

2

When I entered the pub I could sense the general hubbub had stopped abruptly. Two men sitting together at the bar and another man on his own wearing a very loud tie turned to see who had come in. In a corner of the room a couple of youths were playing darts. The one about to throw halted his arm. Only an old man sitting stooped over at a table with a small glass of whiskey in front of him didn't take an interest in me.

My appearance in the pub was bound to cause commotion. Since coming to the village and buying the property, this was the first time I had ventured out among the locals. If I wasn't already a curiosity, the discovery of a human hand on my land would have made me one. Conscious that all eyes were on me, I walked up to the counter. I moved a bar stool to one side, which allowed me to stand against the edge of the counter, and let my gaze wander over the array of drinks stocked behind the bar.

There was horse racing on the television. The barman wore a stained, once white apron tied around his waist. I ordered a Club Orange and watched him ponder for a second. Would he give me an ordinary glass, or one that had been shined? Polished glasses were kept for certain occasions. He glanced at me again. He would have guessed who I was, but I was still a stranger, so I'd probably be eligible for a nice sparkling glass. On the other hand, my order involved only a soft drink. Finally, he chose a polished glass and poured out the mineral.

I forgot that it was the custom here to pay for the drink when served and didn't put my hand in my pocket. The barman didn't comment. He went back to chatting with another customer, and the youths resumed their game of darts. Noise levels returned to normal. I took a sip from my glass and turned around to survey the room. It was long and narrow and shaped like an old-fashioned grocery shop, which in fact it had once been, with just a small part at the end reserved for the licenced premises. In changing times, the economics favoured the bar counter over a shop counter, and the whole property had been turned into a pub.

The barman emptied some ashtrays and gave them a wipe with a damp cloth. He set one down in front of me and said, 'I think it's going to stay nice.'

I regarded him. He had skin the same colour as the ceiling, and I wondered briefly if cigarette smoke would colour a man's face like it did the ceiling. The barman's remark wasn't about the weather. 'Yes, I hope so,' I said.

'Are you just passing through?'

The two men sitting at the bar had stopped talking. Although still watching the horse racing on television, they were listening for my answer.

'No, I live here.'

'Ah,' the barman said, nodding his head. 'You're the man from Australia, the new owner of the old estate.'

'Yup.'

'The house is rundown somewhat.'

'It is that.'

'Will you live there?'

'That's my intention.'

'What's all the baloney about a woman's hand being found in the big meadow?'

Just then from outside, the roar of a motorbike drowned out the conversation in the bar. The noise cut out, and a moment or two later the door opened. A skinny young man came in. I could sense the atmosphere changing. The newcomer came up to the bar and stood on the other side of the two men sitting to my left. The barman greeted him. 'Ah, how's it going there, Soapie?'

Soapie grunted something and said, 'Give me a pint of McArdle's.'

I knew Soapie Crowley from the auction. He took a drink from his pint, looked around the room, and said to no one in particular, 'This place is like a fucking morgue.'

After fidgeting for a couple of minutes and gulping down more beer, he shouted at the youths. 'Here give me a go at those darts. You guys couldn't hit the side of a barn.'

He walked over and one of the lads handed him a set of flights. After positioning himself on the mark that sufficed for a hockey, he fired one of the darts. It bounced off the tyre that surrounded the target put there to protect the wall.

'Not to worry,' he said. 'I'm just warming up.'

He fired another one. This one did hit the board but outside the scoring area. 'Now I'm getting into my stride,' he crowed.

The final dart by chance landed beside the bull's eye. He let out a yahoo. 'What did I tell you?'

'You're very good,' said one of the fellas.

'I am that. Who would like to play me for a quid?'

'Come on, Soapie, let us finish our game,' said the darts player.

Soapie pulled a pound note from his back pocket and held it up in the air. 'I challenge anyone here.'

'Please, Soapie,' said the lad.

'You're all a bunch of yellow bellies,' taunted Soapie. 'Hi Val, another pint there. All this excitement is making me thirsty.'

Soapie made his way over to the counter as the barman poured the pint. 'Give me a half-one of Powers as well.'

'Maybe the pint will be enough, Soapie?' said Val.

'No way,' said Soapie.

'Just one then,' said the barman measuring out a half glass of whiskey.

Soapie lifted the whiskey and swallowed it in one gulp. 'That's how a man throws back a whiskey. How about an oul' song from someone?'

'What song do the Artane band perform when Monaghan plays in Croke Park?' asked one of the customers.

'The way the boys were shaping up last Sunday,' replied his mate, 'I don't think it'll be a huge concern anytime soon.'

'I'm a Monaghan man and I want a Monaghan song,' said Soapie.

'Give us a verse of something, Soapie. Anything will do,' said one of the men.

Soapie, with the pint in his hand, stumbled over to where

the old man was sitting.

'Hi Larry, you've been around a long time. Do you know any Monaghan songs?'

The old man looked at Soapie for a few seconds, and then could just about be heard to say, 'Get your hair cut.'

Soapie's hairstyle resembled a fifties teddy boy. The man with the spectacles at the bar gave his companion a nudge. Soapie shook his head in disgust and went back to the counter. 'Another whiskey,' he demanded of the barman.

'You've had enough.'

'A Monaghan man can hold his drink.'

'Slow up, Soapie,' said Val.

'If I go any slower I'll be arrested for holding up traffic,' said Soapie letting out a guffaw. 'More liquor is what's required.'

'Take a break and come back later,' said the barman.

Soapie steadied himself on his feet and held his head back in mock surprise. 'I can't believe what I'm hearing here.'

'It's for your own good, Soapie.'

'Let me get this right,' said Soapie. 'Are you saying you won't serve me and you'll serve someone from Australia. Someone who has no right to be here.'

'That's not how it is,' said Val.

'You will serve people because they have money and think they can buy up land that rightfully belongs to Monaghan people.'

'Easy on, Soapie,' said the barman.

'Who knows where these guys got the money? Maybe they came by it very handy.'

The man with the loud tie spoke up. 'Hey, young fellow,

go home and sleep it off.'

Soapie let on he didn't hear. He took another swallow from his pint before continuing 'Thieves and murderers don't worry about spending money.'

'Soapie, you're going to have to keep quiet,' said Val.

Soapie pointed his finger accusingly at the men sitting at the bar. 'Everyone knows a woman was murdered in the big meadow. Have you people no pride? Are you going to let outsiders come in and tramp all over us?'

Nobody spoke.

Soapie turned to the barman. 'Val, you have no business serving that foreign bastard.'

The barman didn't reply. He just concentrated on wiping the counter with a cloth and cleaning ashtrays. I set my glass down on the counter and walked slowly over to Soapie who suddenly looked worried.

'Are you referring to me, kid?' I asked, stretching myself to my full six-feet-two.

'You had no right to buy the old estate. It marched our land,' said Soapie full of bluster, but edging backwards as I closed in on him.

'You don't know what you're talking about,' I said.

'I do know,' Soapie managed to stammer.

'Believe me, you don't.'

Val came out from the bar and jammed his way between the two of us. 'I run a respectable pub. Any more from either of you and you're both barred.'

Soapie backed off. Then pointing at Val, he shouted, 'You should be ashamed of yourself siding with interlopers against your neighbours.'

At that he swallowed the last of his pint and said to me, 'This is not the end of it. Just wait and see.' He slammed down the glass on the counter and stormed out the door. Inside the bar, the motor bike could be heard revving up and taking off with a roar.

I walked back to the counter and picked up my glass. The young lads resumed their game of darts. One of the men at the bar said something under his breath to his friend. The loud tie man seemed to be smiling. Val came before me and said, 'What *are* your plans?'

'What do mean my plans?'

'Your plans for living here. It may not be easy.'

'I intend to open a business.'

'A business?'

'Yeah.'

'Where?'

'Right here in Cambroestown.'

'In Cambroestown?'

'Yeah, in Cambroestown.'

'Where in Cambroestown?'

'A couple of hundred yards up the street.'

'Up the street?'

'Yup.'

'What kind of business?'

I swallowed the last of my drink and set it down on the counter. 'A pub business.'

3

When empty, the courtroom smelled like a rural Protestant church, which was unsurprising given it was most likely built by such a congregation. Solid box benches, long narrow windows, and a raised dais for the presiding judge created an austere ambience. It spoke of a time when discipline and continuity were the order of the day.

That afternoon it was stuffy and less sombre than usual. Normally there wouldn't be such a crowd, but this was the annual licensing session so the attendees in court were more diverse. Publicans, pilferers, real estate agents, moneylenders, and one woman charged with attempted murder of her husband, all mingled and waited on their turn.

I sat on the public benches and passed the time observing the proceedings. Beside me a small man with black hair combed over his forehead in a fringe gave me a running commentary. He looked like a schoolmaster, and because of the way he twitched his head to one side and the intensity of his stare, I thought of a robin sitting on a tree watching a gardener dig a hole.

The Dublin legal firm that looked after my affairs had advised me to engage a barrister. There would surely be objections, they said, and I would need expert representation. I watched solicitors applying for a late-opening bar explain to the magistrate that since a substantial meal would be served on these occasions, people should be allowed to have a glass of wine with their food as in any civilised society.

'Probably the meal in most cases will be a chicken leg and a few greasy chips,' commented the robin man. 'And there won't be much wine consumed. Around here, wine is for old ladies and the odd French tourist.'

After the late extensions, the magistrate granted a raft of applications for betting shop licences. They came under the heading of a turf accountant's premises. The word gambling was never mentioned.

'All that stuff to do with licences is just a bluff to circumvent the law,' remarked my companion.

'Why don't they change the law and be upfront about it?' I asked.

'Be upfront about it? You're in Ireland, man.'

The woman on the murder charge was granted continuing bail, and eventually the court recorder called out, 'Joseph Walker, application for change of ownership of licensed premises.'

'That's me, Your Honour,' I said, standing up.

The magistrate, Judge Flannery, was a slight man with a pale complexion. He bent over to speak to the court recorder, half-moon glasses on the tip of his nose.

'Jesus, you're the guy in the big house all the talk is about,' said the little robin man.

'What talk?'

'Human heads and hands found in fields. Dismembered bodies all over the place. There hasn't been so much gossip in Cambroestown since the signing of the treaty.'

'Are you not afraid to sit beside me?'

'Above all places, I should be safe in a court of law.'

I laughed and said, 'You have a point.'

'I'm Benjamin, but most people call me Jack,' he said, putting out his hand to shake mine.

'Are you also looking for a licence?' I asked.

It was Jack's turn to laugh. 'No, my hobby is courtrooms.'

'That's a strange hobby.'

'Some people join Toastmasters. Some people race pigeons. I like courtrooms.'

'You should have been a barrister.'

'Would a pigeon fancier want to be a pigeon?'

The judge stopped speaking to his clerk. He peered at the court over his spectacles. 'The application forms seem to be in order. Who is representing the applicant?'

My friend nudged me. Indicating the judge, he said, ' Watch him. Flannery likes attention, and I hope you don't propose any ungodly ideas. He's well-known to be deeply involved in Catholic affairs.'

A man rose and said, 'I am, Your Honour.'

My barrister was tall and bald except for one lock of fair hair that crossed the crown of his head. When he bent down to look at papers on his desk, the single strand fell to one side and had to be fixed in place.

Jack nodded towards the lawyer. 'Lanky Larry is up against it today.'

'Why?'

'Just wait.'

'Do you know my barrister?'

'I know them all.'

A man with an air of someone used to the limelight stood up and stated in an authoritative voice, 'I wish to object to this application.'

'That's what I mean about Lanky being up against it,' said Jack. 'That guy, Branighan, is local, but he's also one of the big cheeses in the law library up in Dublin. When I see him back down here it's not hard to guess somebody's determined to get their way.'

'What about my man?'

'I have seen him in action before. He isn't bad.'

'And the big cheese opposing us?'

'I call him Mighty Mo, because he's from Monaghan. Believe me, he's good.'

The judge began speaking. 'When I look at the eminent jurists involved in this case, I might be forgiven if I were to think I had been elevated to some higher court. It isn't often this humble little courtroom is host to such celebrated, not to say expensive, legal expertise.'

Jack leaned over, 'He loves a bit of attention and showing who's in charge. Pray he doesn't take umbrage at your man's accent.'

'Our application is in order and any grounds for it being opposed can only be spurious and ill-conceived,' said my lawyer.

'Ah, Mr Cleary,' said the judge, looking expansively around the room as if to give his mind some momentary relaxation. 'I often wondered if you are related to the well-known O'Connell Street people.'

Lanky Larry rose to his feet. 'Unfortunately not, Your Honour.'

'It's probably your accent that brought that to my mind.'

Jack nudged me again. 'I told you. He has a chip on his shoulder about moneyed people, especially if they have a cultured accent.'

I thought about how I must sound to people.

'Perhaps,' said the judge to Mighty Mo, 'you will state your objections to the licence transfer.'

The barrister stood up, straightened his shoulders and joined his hands behind his back. 'My clients' objections are three in number.'

The judge interrupted him. 'It may be of interest to the court to know who your clients are.'

'Of course, Your Honour. I have been engaged by a number of concerned local citizens who have banded together, so that the village of Cambroestown may be allowed to retain its natural charm, and not be sullied by outside entrepreneurs coming in and changing the ambience of the community.'

'There's the concerned local citizens,' whispered Jack, pointing at the Crowleys and Val Donaghy the publican. I hadn't seen them come in, but they were standing together at the back of the court.

'Please continue,' said the judge.

'Thank you, Your Honour.' The lawyer oozed self-belief. 'As I have already stated, we have three main concerns relating to this application. The premises in question are part of the old Cambroestown estate, and as such passed over to the new owner at the recent sale of same. The building that at one time had been a licensed premises has been neglected, even more so than the big house, and in fact has been lying derelict for this past quarter century. To grant this application would therefore be akin to the issuing of a new licence. This is concern one.

'Two. A new licensed premises is not needed in the area. The existing one barely survives. If there were to be a new pub then neither of them could generate enough business.

'Three. It is wrong that outsiders with no previous stake in the area should be allowed to come in and skim off profits that arose from the labour of generations of local people.

'Finally, although it does not form part of my official objections, I might just add as an addendum that there are many rumours concerning the finding of human remains on the applicant's recently acquired lands.'

Mighty Mo sat down. The judge shook his head. 'Mr Branighan, I should not need to remind you that a court of law is not a suitable place to be articulating rumours, especially when they have no bearing on the case before the court.'

'I stand corrected,' said Mighty Mo.

'Fair play to the judge,' I said to my friend.

Jack looked at me. 'This is getting more interesting by the minute.'

'What did you think of the judge shooting down the barrister?'

'You don't understand,' Jack replied. 'It's more devious than that. Branighan knew he'd be shot down and was prepared for the reprimand, but he has reminded the judge of the rumours concerning you, and that cannot be undone.'

The judge turned to my barrister. 'I presume you can counter these objections.'

'Yes indeed, Your Honour. This is not a new licence. These premises have been licensed to sell alcohol and tobacco for the past one hundred years.'

Mo was on his feet. 'Your Honour, it has been closed for almost half of that time.'

My man hadn't sat down. 'I would remind my friend of the law in this regard. If the premises in question has been opened one day in the year for business, then the licence shall not become redundant. These conditions have been adhered to.'

'He has him there,' Jack whispered to me. 'All it needed was the door of the place to be left open one day in the year. Who can say if that happened or not? And anyway, the solicitors for the estate would have made sure it occurred to keep the licence extant.'

The judge turned to Lanky Larry. 'Will you address the second objection?'

Lanky fixed his strand of hair in place again. 'If it please Your Honour, we live in a capitalist society. Competition is the essence of capitalism. Russia is not capitalist. It is a communist country where there is no competition. It is a godless pagan country. Religion is banned. They don't recognise God in heaven who will one day judge us all. Is that the sort of Ireland we want? We must have competition if we are not to drift towards socialism, and all its attendant ills, not least of which is atheism.'

'Two up,' said Jack excitedly. 'And Flannery is milking

the confrontation for all it's worth. He thinks he's the Lord Chief Justice letting the two barristers slug it out.'

'It's not two up yet,' I said.

Mighty Mo still looked confidant. 'Your Honour, there's no competition if both parties go to the wall, what's the point of that?'

The judge looked to Larry for a reply.

'Your Honour, if I may use the example of two men in the boxing ring. There will be a winner and a loser. That's competition as it should be. The best man wins. So it is in business. Can anything be more fair?'

'Flannery was an excellent lightweight boxer at college,' said Jack. 'Your man has done his homework. It's definitely two up now.'

Mo was quickly on his feet again. His voice had a more urgent tone. 'Your Honour, all of this is irrelevant.'

'Here it comes,' Jack whispered to me. 'He's gearing himself up for a big speech.'

I glanced at Jack. A football spectator wouldn't be so engrossed.

The barrister drew in a long deep breath through his nose. 'By the mercy and goodness of the great creator, Your Honour, I have been born and bred in this most wonderful county.'

Judge Flannery made himself more comfortable.

'Mo thinks he's Micheál Mac Liammóir,' said Jack.

'"What relevance has that to the case here before us today?" you may ask. It is relevant because it gives me the right to speak as I do about things here in Monaghan. This is a privilege my learned friend from Dublin does not enjoy.

It is not his fault of course that he speaks with an accent that is foreign to us. It is not his fault that his background is alien to our way of life here. Perhaps it is not his fault if tonight he will be back home wining and dining with people who better understand his way of being. But it is his fault if he comes among us and tries to tell us about fairness.'

Mo took a drink from a glass of water and raised his voice. 'Because, Your Honour, this case is all about fairness.' He paused again. 'Let us begin at the beginning.

'Cambroestown House has been with us for generations, employing and providing work for people. The village itself came into being because of the big house. Local people got employment and the owners of the estate had their needs attended to. In a way it was a happy marriage, but like all marriages it had to be worked at. There were tough times. Times when the villagers didn't have enough to eat. Times when their children went to school hungry. Times when people couldn't afford a doctor and died as a result. Your Honour, local businesses helped out at such times. Those who made the laws in faraway Dublin didn't care. Sometimes rich people with fancy accents would turn up to survey the situation and then go away again. To be fair, as a general rule the big house occupants helped out as best they could during such hardships, but they also had their own trials.'

The barrister paused for a few seconds to let his words sink in.

'Great stuff,' said Jack to me, excitedly. 'I'm afraid you're in trouble.'

I didn't reply.

'Your Honour, it cannot be fair that in these times of relative plenty, an outsider, nay even a foreigner, should be allowed to come and feast on whatever meagre good times that now prevail. It cannot be fair that someone who has no knowledge of the hardships this community lived through for generations should now suddenly impose himself upon it.'

Mighty Mo stopped again. Then with his face red with passion, he shouted, 'It cannot be fair that a business that served the community in good times and bad should go to the wall to satisfy the greed of someone who arrives here from *six thousand miles* away.'

His voice dropped. 'Our beloved bard, Monaghan's very own Paddy Kavanagh, describes us as creatures made of clay, or as that most holy of books puts it, dust from dust. The people I represent spring from Cambroestown dust and are fashioned from that very same "stony grey soil". That, Your Honour, with all its attendant consequences, is the crucial difference between them and the one seeking the new licence. I ask you to dismiss this application.'

The judge took a deep breath and addressed the room. 'The reputation of the objectors' advocate is indeed well earned. His rhetoric is compelling and his disputations, I have to conclude, are difficult to ignore. However, in the interests of justice, transparency, and the concept upon which the arguments in this case have concentrated, fairness, it is only proper that I should allow the applicant's lawyer a final say before I announce my decision.'

Mighty Mo consulted with his junior, a smug smile on his face. I watched my barrister intently. I had a pretty good idea how he was going to respond. Jack twitched his head almost continuously. Lanky Larry fastidiously fixed his hair and shuffled papers as if searching for something. Finally, he picked out a document, walked up to the judge, and handed it to him.

The judge looked over his glasses at the room. Everybody had their eyes on him. Then he read the note. His expression didn't change. He paused, lifted his head and stared into space. After a few seconds he gave his head a slight shake and handed the piece of paper to the court recorder, telling him to pass it to the concerned citizens' lawyer.

Mighty Mo stood up to take it. He glanced at the document, and the expression on his face changed, before he plopped back down on his seat, visibly stunned. He kept staring at it in disbelief.

'Jesus, what's happening?' whispered Jack.

The judge began speaking. 'Let it be recorded that the applicant has produced a birth certificate which proves he has been born in the county of Monaghan. In fact in the very house that has been the focus of attention here. His birth name is Cambroe. Joseph Cambroe. Cambroe of Cambroestown House. His lineage can no doubt be traced much further than most people in this room. I will grant his application. Court is adjourned.'

The room was silent. Jack turned and grasped my hand, saying, 'Congratulations. My father worked as groundsman on the Cambroestown estate, and I still live in the village. I will be honoured to be there at the opening, or should I say, the reopening of your bar.'

I shook his hand warmly. 'You have my invitation. Will you join me for a cup of coffee?'

'I'd be happy to.'

There were only a few people in the little café when we entered, but they all turned to look at me. We ordered the coffee, and Jack was just saying that I wouldn't find it plain sailing when Soapie burst in through the door. He made straight for our table.

'You will never serve a fucking drink in that dump, you Australian bastard,' he roared before backing out of the door again.

Jack looked at me while stirring his coffee. 'Do you see what I mean?'

4

The number of Land Rovers in the car park suggested an Irish Farmers Association meeting was taking place in the hotel. In the foyer, farming men stood around in twos and threes talking country talk. I felt out of place. Many of them stared. One man in particular wearing a tartan cap precariously on the side of his head and with a lit cigarette stuck to his lower lip seemed fascinated by me. When he got home he would be able to say that he saw the man all the talk was about. But Maura, the hotel receptionist, never treated me as an object of curiosity and always had a welcome. Her face lit up when she saw me. 'Hello, my Australian friend,' she said. 'Where are your wellies?'

'I don't see anyone in wellies,' I replied.

'Maybe the farmers don't wear them anymore. It's all machinery now. A quiz question for you,' said Maura, leaning her forearms on the reception desk. 'Quizzes are very popular around here. Why are they called wellingtons?'

'How would I know why they are called wellingtons? There's a Wellington in Australia and one in New Zealand. Maybe they were invented there or something.'

Maura tut-tutted. 'Not good.'

'Is this a hotel or a school?' I said.

Maura straightened herself up in an exaggerated businesslike pose. 'We offer the finest cuisine and are famed far and wide for our hospitality to the public, sir.'

'I'm glad to hear that,' I said. 'I'm tired of cooking for myself and decided to let someone else make my dinner for a change.'

'You need a woman.'

'Are you making me an offer?'

Maura laughed, highlighting the dimples on her cheeks. 'I don't know about Australia, but in Monaghan you have to woo and court a woman for a long time. Then if she marries you she'll make your dinner . . . if you're lucky.'

'I'd be ready for it by the time I had done all that. What would you recommend from the menu?'

'I have never seen you order anything other than steak.'

'I'm really an Irishman, don't forget.'

'Why are you asking me then what you will have?'

'Don't I always ask you?'

'Yeah, and every time I wonder why you bother when you have already decided. Take a seat in the dining room and I'll put in your order.'

'Would you have time to join me?' I asked.

She looked taken aback at the abruptness of the invitation and covered her mouth with her hand in surprise. After a little hesitation, she said she would join me in the lounge for a drink when I had eaten. In the dining room, every plate I saw had steak on it except one, which I took to be fish, and this was for a lady. Custard and apple tart seemed to be the dessert of choice. When I was in Australia, banoffee pie was all the rage. I wondered if there would be a demand for it here.

After an excellent steak and potatoes, I moved into the lounge, ordered a club orange and surveyed the room. A couple of men occupied chairs at another table with pints of Guinness in front of them. Beside them a party of four, perhaps a young couple taking in-laws out for the evening, were chatting. A rotund priest shared an alcove with a man and woman, and two solitary men sat at either end of the bar watching an episode of *Bonanza* on television. The red carpet on the lounge floor needed cleaning, but the soft lighting concealed the dust. Easy chairs in colours that matched the carpet looked shabby.

I didn't notice the man approach me from behind. 'Only a foreigner wouldn't use a glass,' he said. 'Here it is not really acceptable to drink from the bottle.'

'Why is that?'

The stranger pulled over a chair and sat down beside me. 'I don't know. Maybe it stems from the time when we didn't have tumblers.'

'What's a tumbler?'

'A glass for holding beer.'

'That's interesting.'

'You don't know me, Joey?'

I stared at the man. He was medium height with a bulging beer belly and almost bald. One arm hanging by his side ended above the wrist. 'My God. Mickey Patton.'

'The one and only,' said Mickey, reaching out his single hand. 'Welcome home.'

I shook Mickey's hand, saying, 'Thank you.'

'There was talk of somebody buying the old place. Then

I heard about your licence application, but I still wasn't sure it was you until I saw your crooked finger.'

'My father said it would always be a means of identifying me. But I'm sorry for not recognising you, especially because of the hand.'

'It's a long time ago now,' said Mickey.

'It seemed to take forever for them to get the wall off you where it had you pinned down. I can still remember your screams ringing in my ears.'

'Yeah.'

'It must have been horrific.'

'I wasn't out of hospital long when you suffered your own horror.'

He didn't seem to want to discuss what he went through. Was that because I was responsible for having shoved him off the wall as a childish prank, and in the process caused the loose stones to fall on top of him? 'Yeah, we had to make a quick flit.'

Mickey folded his arms across his chest by holding the severed stump. 'How are you anyway?' he said. 'I know it's a long time ago, the fire and all, but it wasn't right what happened.'

'Yes, it was a long time ago.'

'They were different times then.'

'Yeah.'

'The people involved must surely all be dead by now,' he said.

'You have lived here all your life. It must be common knowledge who they were. Or at least rumoured.'

'Rumours and facts are different.'

'Sometimes they're the same.'

Mickey looked around the room. When he spoke his voice was lower. 'What am I hearing from you, Josie?'

'Curiosity,' I said. 'Surely I have a right to be curious about who was responsible?'

'It's usually best not to stir the well.'

Just then Maura came over.

'Ah, here comes the beautiful Maura,' said Mickey. She sat down beside me, and he asked, 'You two know each other?'

'Don't be jealous now, Mickey,' said Maura.

'Now, would you give me a reason to be jealous?'

'Sure you know I wouldn't,' said Maura.

'Yeah,' said Mickey. 'I believe you.'

'Anyway, there's rumours you have a romantic attraction elsewhere that you keep quiet about,' said Maura.

'If I went to Knock they would say I have a girlfriend there,' said Mickey.

'It wasn't Knock I heard you were in, and it wasn't saying the rosary you were at.'

'If people were saying their prayers they wouldn't have time to be talking about me,' he said, and he got up to leave.

I asked Maura about Knock. She said it was in County Mayo, that Our Lady had appeared there and people went to it on pilgrimage, the same as rich people go to Lourdes. Mickey had never married. He had lived on his own since the woman who reared him died. He had looked after her into her old age. Maura thought he had a hang-up to do with the loss of his arm.

'He covers the reception desk when it's quiet, but he has

a bit of a *grá* for me,' she said.

I asked her how she felt about him.

'No way,' she said, 'and anyway here things aren't that simple.'

I didn't pursue the issue. 'When we were children, he and I played together,' I said.

'It was quick of him to recognise you.'

'He's probably been looking out for me since the auction and the licence application.'

'There must be others of your generation still around,' said Maura.

'Yes, there has to be.'

'You will meet them I'm sure.' Maura got up and went over to the bar. She had nice legs. I watched her ask the barman for more orange in her vodka. When she returned, she said, 'Now, tell me all about Australia.'

'What do you want to know?'

'Is it as hot as they say? Is everyone very rich? Do people go to mass? Do the ladies wear mini-skirts?' She laughed. 'Do the men wear wellies? I want to know everything.'

'Whoa there,' I said. 'I'm not an encyclopaedia.'

'You've been there, and there's something else.'

'What's that?'

'Have you a wife, or have you never been married?'

I hesitated for a second. 'Yes, I've been married. What about you? How come you have never married? Although I'm just assuming that.'

'You're assuming right. Do you know what it's like to live in a small country town where everybody knows how many times you turned in the bed at night?'

My mind flashed to places where you wouldn't see a living soul for days. 'No I can't say I do.'

'If you look crooked at a guy you're going to marry him. If he's well-to-do you're marrying him for the money. If he's poor you have no sense. If you don't get married then you're desperate for a man and cannot get one, either that or you're a little bit funny. If you don't go out with fellas you're stuck up, if you do, you're the talk of the town. If you miss a couple of days at work, either you have a serious illness, or you're a lazy no-good taking advantage of your employer.'

Maura paused, and stirred the ice in her vodka with a swizzle stick 'The topic of conversation never changes. In the spring it's about the bad weather and nothing growing. In the summer it's about the bad weather and not getting the silage cut. In the autumn it's about the bad weather and the harvest being lost, and in the winter it's about the bad weather and the shortage of fodder.'

I laughed at her laments.

'Is that enough,' she said, 'or do you want to hear more?'

'That'll keep me going,' I said.

She wondered why I didn't drink alcohol, and I replied that I was giving it a breather for a while. She had another vodka and orange. Mickey had been moving in and out of the lounge. He walked past saying, 'Don't be making advances on the local talent.'

Maura drank more vodka. 'You never answered my question.'

'What question?'

'About being married.'

'I did answer. I said I had married.'

'And?'

'And what?'

'Jesus! It would be easier to get butter from churned milk than to get a straight answer from you. Why did you change your name? I heard about the court case.'

There was no point going into details, so I just said, 'Things were tough when my parents landed in Australia. They didn't want what happened at home to be associated with them, so they called themselves by a different name. But my real name is Cambroe.'

Maura was about to reply when she abruptly leaned towards me and said in a whisper, 'Don't look now, but the Fling Devlin has just come in.'

I didn't look around. 'Who the hell is the Fling Devlin?'

'Fling is his nickname. His real name is Phillip. He's been the local TD for as long as I can remember.'

'What's a TD?'

'Maybe it's called Member of Parliament in your country. You would think at this stage he would let some younger guy in that would maybe do something for the area instead of spouting about it at every election.'

I glanced over at the man. He was tall with white hair. As he walked over to sit down he had an obvious limp. I stared at him.

'He was big in the Old IRA,' said Maura.

'When Sergeant Love was taking me in for a statement he told me about the IRA. But you call it the Old IRA.'

'What did you think of Love?' said Maura.

'Why do you ask?'

'Oh, no reason.'

'I thought he was non-committal like all policemen, so why do want to know my opinion of him?'

Maura smiled – she had a beautiful smile. 'It's always good to get to know how the law operates in a small town. Anyway the IRA were the army that fought the British in the War of Independence. But following a treaty with the Brits in which the six northern counties stayed in the UK and the rest became independent, there was a split in the IRA which resulted in civil war. The side that lost the civil war maintained that they were the true IRA, and it's their descendants today who keep up the fight to have the border between the two parts of Ireland removed, and so create a united Irish Republic.'

'Where does Fling Devlin fit into this?'

'Many on the side that lost the civil war eventually went along with the treaty and became part of the establishment. Fling was a member of that group. They are known as the Old IRA and are scorned by the those who are still prepared to resist, who have never sold out as they would see it.'

'So, Love?'

'Today's IRA are outlawed but people are sometimes ambiguous towards them. It's Love's job to know things and I wondered if he suspects you of having an interest in IRA activities. Why are you shaking your head?'

'For a lady who works as a hotel receptionist, rather than a newspaper reporter, you have a great interest in what's going on with me, the sergeant, the local MP, and the entire community.'

Again she smiled. It was worth teasing her just to see it. 'Let me fill you in, Mr Australian. I am the exact same as everyone else in this town. Some Russian sputnik in the sky doesn't affect our life, but the local sergeant can. This is not America. We don't have black marches here and people singing we will overcome, and as for drugs the nearest thing we have to marijuana is magic mushrooms . . . which isn't bad,' she added with a laugh.

Then she leaned over and whispered, 'Watch this.' Mickey had come into the lounge. He went straight over to the TD Fling Delvin and adopted a deferential attitude. They started chatting.

'Do you see Mickey licking up to the Fling?' said Maura. 'He must be looking for something.'

'Like what?' I asked, curious.

'It could be about planning permission, a pension, a job for someone, you wouldn't know. He's always been a great Fling man. I think he just likes to be seen talking to him because he thinks he's someone important.'

'A VIP,' I said.

Maura just grunted something. Mickey left the Fling and came over to our table.

'I see you're hobnobbing with the big people,' said Maura.

Mickey asked if I knew who the Fling was.

'Yes, Maura told me.'

'Do you know he was wounded during the troubles?'

'By who?'

'He was on the anti-treaty side,' said Mickey.

'It might have been his wife,' said Maura, her tone dripping with sarcasm.

'No, he was definitely wounded,' said Mickey. 'He's

famous for it – the last man to be shot in the civil war. They called a ceasefire the very same day.'

'He has obviously made a big thing of it,' I said.

'He's one decent man,' said Mickey. 'If you need something done, Josie, he won't let you down.'

'Who's covering reception?' asked Maura.

'I am,' said Mickey. 'I better be getting back.'

When he had gone, Maura said, 'Don't take anything at face value. You never can tell what's going on. Mickey mightn't even like the Fling for all we know.'

'That's funny talk.'

'You have no idea. In spite of appearances, not everything is always on the surface in this green land. Like a duck's legs there could be a lot going on underneath the water. Mickey could really admire the Fling or he could be putting on a show, and the great thing about it is the Fling also knows that. If you're not sure, it's better to just think things and say nothing.'

I put my hand on my heart. 'I promise to keep my mouth tight as a clam and say nothing.'

Maura opened her handbag and took out a compact set. She opened it and looked at herself in the little mirror. 'You don't have to say anything. You're the talk of the locality. First buying Cambroestown, and then bits of a woman being dug up in one of the fields.'

'I know I have caused a lot of stir buying the old place, but I'm not responsible for the dead woman being discovered.'

Maura put away the mirror. 'It's the two events happening at the same time.'

'Yeah, that was unfortunate.'

'The Crowleys thought they would get the farm.'

'They didn't.'

'That's the problem, and some people might agree with them.'

'What do *you* say?'

'Amn't I after telling you? Whatever you say, say nothing.'

I smiled and stood up, telling her that nature called. Coming back from the toilet I saw that Maura was having an animated discussion with the barman. He moved off when I sat down. 'What was all that about?' I asked.

'The cheek of him. I went out with him a couple of times. Now he thinks he owns me.'

'Was he annoyed at you talking to me?'

'He was complaining that just because people are rich they think they can come here and get anything they want.'

'Oh.'

'I told him I had a mind of my own.'

I glanced around the room. 'There doesn't seem to be much happening here.'

'There'll be less happening around Cambroestown, if we ignore dead women being dug up in fields.'

'What are people saying about that?'

'All kinds of things. You're a serial killer who murdered women in Australia, which is why you changed your name. The dead woman had some connection with your family when they lived in Ireland. You took the hand home in a suitcase because it belonged to your wife, and buried it on the land.'

'Why would I report it if that was the case?'

'You thought if you reported it that would keep you in the clear.'

'Jesus!'

'There are also suggestions that the Crowleys, particularly Soapie, had something to do with it to scare you off.'

'Is there nobody saying that it's just a coincidence – the hand being found and me buying the land?'

Maura laughed at me. 'What would be the craic, fun to you, if the two events were just a coincidence?'

'Are you not afraid of me?'

'You're hardly going to kill me and cut me to pieces here in the lounge.'

'There's a nice lake-walk out at Cambroestown. How about you and I going for a dander around it?'

Maura was just about to take a sip from her drink, but stopped. 'Wait a minute. You're asking me to go for a walk with you alone in the dark?'

'It's a nice night.'

She stared at me. 'Ah, now I know you're just testing me.'

'No, I'm in earnest.'

'Would you kill me and butcher me up?'

I laughed. 'Lots of people would have seen me with you, so it would be too risky.'

'If I go with you, Josie Cambroe, you better not kill me, do you hear?'

'I hear you. Get your coat.'

As we were getting into the car I noticed a man parked close by. He seemed to be taking an interest in us. I started up the engine, and while manoeuvring out of the car park I made sure to shine my headlights on the other car. Sergeant Love was sitting in it.

Once or twice on the way home I got the impression we were being followed. Lights on a vehicle behind us would appear and then just as quickly fall away again. It was the same vehicle because there was a sidelight missing. Would a police car have a sidelight missing? An unmarked police car might as part of its cover.

When we got to Cambroestown House it was almost as bright as day. The lake water, crystal clear, gently lapped at the edges. In the shallow reeds a rustling sound could be heard. It might have been water hens or ducks, but I had a feeling there was someone hiding there. An owl hooted in a tree. I bent down, picked up a pebble and threw it into the reeds, letting Maura think I was just tossing it into the water. There was no reaction from the undergrowth, but little ripples spread out from the disturbed surface.

'Every action one makes,' I said, keeping up the pretence of just idly firing the stone, 'no matter how tiny, causes waves that spread out to who knows where.'

'Then big actions must make bigger ripples,' said Maura.

We held hands as we walked. A fox suddenly darted across our path from the shadows causing Maura to startle. I put my arms around her and looked over her head as I held her. There was no indication of any human activity.

'Since I arrived here, you're maybe the only one who hasn't looked at me as if I had horns.'

'If you had horns it might be that much easier,' said Maura.

'Why?'

'I would know what I was dealing with.'

We went back to the house. By the time we arrived the moon had risen high in the sky painting the outside walls in soft cream and lighting up the lawn where the snowdrops and crocuses were dying off. It created shadows among the chestnut trees now coming into leaf, and caused the dew on the daffodils lining each side of the driveway to sparkle. All was still, except for the mass of yellow heads swaying in the gentle breeze, creating an eerie illusion that the drive itself was swaying. I turned and led the way up the steps to the front door.

A hessian bag with something inside it lay in the portico. The opening was tied with a piece of string. The bag was heavy. I undid the knot and turned the bag upside down. A dead sheepdog, its legs cut off, rolled out onto the concrete. Maura recoiled in horror. I stared at the animal. It wasn't old, and judging by the shiny hair it was unlikely to have been sick. It had died from a wound to the head, almost certainly a gunshot.

5

I carried out a tour of pubs and lounges around the area to help me decide on the type of premises I wanted. Clearly the most successful ones had a lounge big enough for bands to provide entertainment. The busiest also had a little dance floor in the centre. From my observations, after hearing them play in several venues, the most popular group was an outfit called The Country Cowboys. So my plans for the pub included a spacious lounge with a little dance floor, a side bar for regular customers, and I would book The Country Cowboys for my opening night.

At the same time, I intended to get the pub contractors to carry out some improvements to the big house. Although new doors and windows had been installed by previous owners, the original contours hadn't changed. It was still the same square Georgian house built in the late 1700s by my ancestor Major William Cambroe for his new bride.

I recalled the house as draughty and almost impossible to heat. My parents weren't rich. The wealth lay in the lands that went with the house, although during their tenure the acreage diminished. At its peak, the estate constituted over 800 acres, a substantial area of woodland and a lake. I remembered a boathouse on the lakeshore for storing little boats used by the gentry for fishing. The lake's primary function was to provide a constant supply of water to drive the grinding mills in the farmyard. Now the whole area had been turned into a public amenity by the county council. My purchase consisted of thirty acres, the big house, and the derelict pub in the village. The village itself comprised a post office, a small supermarket, Donaghy's bar, a ladies hairdressers, a garage with petrol pumps, a farm machinery business, and at the edge of the hamlet, a little garden centre run by Ms Gormley, an Englishwoman who had settled in the area. Beside the garden centre stood a thatched cottage with a sign in the window saying, 'Teas Served,' although it wasn't open for business. Another couple of derelict buildings were formerly part of the estate, just as the whole village had once been.

Maura kept me filled-in on the local gossip. One evening she told me about a barn dance that was taking place. The dance, a fundraising event by the local amateur dramatic society, was to be held in Mulligan's loft. She said it would be good for me to get more involved in the community by attending. These were the people who would become my customers when I opened the pub. She would come with me. I bought a new suit for the event.

As we climbed the old concrete steps leading to the loft, the smell of warm cow dung wafted up. Underneath was a byre for ten milking cows, a suckling calf house, and a dairy for cooling and storing the milk. I paid the admission fee of ten shillings each and was given a ticket that would enter us into the various raffles to be held during the proceedings.

'I don't know why I'm taking one,' I said. 'I never win

anything.'

'Maybe your luck has changed,' said Maura.

The loft, usually filled with bales of hay, had a timber floor. Folding chairs were placed around the walls. On a little stage two brothers played piano-accordions accompanied by a lady who just now was rubbing a fiddle bow over and back on a block of rosin. Maura pointed to furtive movements in the corner where one of the guys was selling poitín. She didn't have to tell me what poitín was. Moonshine was the same the world over. I could have taught the manufacturers a thing or two. Soapie Crowley was there among a gang of youths.

The room was full of people dancing 'The Waves of Tory'. We made our way among them. I saw two vacant chairs and was guiding Maura in their direction when she tugged my arm and said, 'I think two Crowley brothers are in those other seats.'

Soapie's siblings were out dancing and their vacant chairs were close to where I had intended sitting. 'I don't mind how close I am to the Crowleys. They can pop down on my knee if they want,' I said.

Maura just shook her head.

After a few minutes taking in the surroundings, I told Maura that not everyone was interested in dancing.

'How do you know?' she asked.

I pointed to two groups of lads who stood in opposite corners of the room whispering and colluding with each other while glaring across the small divide between them. 'That's a stand-off if ever I saw one.'

'For such a quiet man you seem to know a lot about

possible rows,' said Maura.

'But am I correct?'

'Last Sunday a huge fight erupted at a football game between Cambroestown and Ballypatrick,' she said. 'The lads are supporters from the opposing sides.'

'Well, it's no concern of ours.'

'You're correct about that as well. Come on out on the floor. Are we here to dance or to gossip about the neighbours?'

Maura persuaded me to attempt an old-time waltz, but I coped better with 'The Siege of Ennis', which involved couples in a line advancing and retreating, representing an army attacking a town and being beaten back – something I found strange. The dynamics of a vicious battle where people were killed and maimed had been transformed into a joyful rollicking jig. Maybe I was missing something. Raffles were held – I wasn't lucky – and then food was served. Everyone got an empty cup, and ladies went around with huge pots of tea and plates of ham and chicken sandwiches. Afterwards some people were called up to sing. The songs were mostly republican ballads, and one young girl sang 'Noreen Bawn' very beautifully.

Mickey Patton's lack of a hand didn't stop him holding Maura close when doing a slow waltz. Afterwards Maura said, 'He held me that tight I thought I would have smothered.'

I asked her why Kevin the hotel barman hadn't asked her to dance. Had he lost interest in her?

'He's huffing because I'm with you,' she said.

'At least Soapie is in good form,' I said, watching the

Crowley lad and his mate. They were doing some kind of two-hand jig to what Maura called a sixteen-hand reel.

'He won't win any ballroom dancing competitions,' she said.

Just then a commotion began in the moonshine corner. A young fellow fell back into a set of dancers. He had obviously been struck or pushed.

'That's it started now,' said Maura. 'The Cambroestown and Ballypatrick lads are renewing hostilities.'

At the bottom end of the hall a general melee had broken out. Some people were bent on attacking the enemy while others attempted to separate the parties. The confusion was such that only the protagonists would have any idea who was who. 'It'll burn itself out in a little while,' she said.

'You don't seem concerned.'

'If the lads didn't get to display their bravery and fighting talents it wouldn't be classed a good night.'

'Oh yeah?'

'It's always the guys who don't dance who are involved in a ruckus. It's their way of getting notice and making up for their lack of skills on the dance floor.'

A heave of bodies made its way up the middle of the room. I spotted Soapie running towards me with both fists closed and at the ready. Due to his surprise attack I was flung back against the wall. The two other brothers joined in on the assault. I fell to the floor with the Crowleys on top of me. But in their eagerness to inflict damage they were getting in each other's way. I stuck up one hand and grabbed a pair of testicles which I squeezed and yanked at the same time. There was a loud squeal, and all of a sudden the weight on top of me eased enough for me to twist my head a little. The back of someone's leg was pushed against my mouth. A guy who had been in a lot of scrapes once told me, 'Every part of your body is a weapon if you know how to use it.'

I bit the leg as hard as I could. This resulted in another howl and the weight got still lighter. I jumped up onto my feet just as Soapie rushed forward again. I stepped aside, and as he missed his target I gave him a thump on the back of his neck. The strike left him floored and practically unconscious. Another of the brothers jumped on me. I raised my knee and rammed it into his groin. He buckled and went down with his head touching the floor like a Muslim praying to Mecca. The third brother hesitated.

'Come ahead,' I teased him, while at the same time feeling a little bit guilty. It was too easy. These guys had no experience. However, his good sense prevailed and instead of attempting physical force he accused me of beating up his brothers.

'I'm reporting you to the guards for assault,' he shouted at me in an attempt to excuse his lack of courage.

Meanwhile the original scuffle had petered out. I could feel dampness on my face. Maura took my arm and made me sit down. 'It's just a nose bleed,' she said holding a handkerchief to my nostrils.

'Look at my new clothes,' I said. They were splattered with blood.

Some men helped the Crowleys limp away, and a steward got up on the stage and announced a resumption of the dance starting with a haymakers jig.

Jack, my friend from the courtroom, came over and

asked me if I was ok. I told him I had been minding my own business when the fight started.

'It's always the way,' he said. 'Once a racket starts people feel they are entitled to have their own particular disagreements sorted out. The initial shemozzle gave Soapie a licence to attack you.'

'I didn't think he needed an excuse.'

'He'd be accused of starting the trouble if there wasn't a scuffle going on. But the Crowleys probably knew coming here there would be a fracas at some stage.'

'You might have warned me,' I said to Maura. 'I would have worn something different.'

'So do you have a special outfit for events like this?'

I looked at her. 'I never know if you're serious or not.'

'I never know when *you're* serious. You're a strange man, Josie. You don't talk about yourself.' Maura scrutinised my face. 'Are you ok?'

'Yeah, I'm fine.'

'You're lucky you weren't hurt.'

'I'd say it's the Crowleys who are lucky,' said Jack.

'Come on,' said Maura. 'Let's dance. I'm going to teach you the barn dance.'

'What's that?'

'The English stole the beat and called it a quickstep. The Americans transformed it into jiving. Here we go, one, two, three.'

Half an hour later it was as if there had never been any disturbance. People danced, talked and enjoyed themselves. Mickey Patton came over and said goodbye. It struck me how much of a tragedy losing his arm had been. Even at a dance you really need two arms. Kevin also left. He didn't come near us.

'He's still in a huff,' said Maura. 'He's afraid he's gone out of fashion with me.'

I looked her in the eye. 'Has he?'

'What do you mean?'

'Can I be the latest fashion?'

Maura looked away. 'Josie, I never know what to make of you.'

'That's not an answer.'

'My father says to always check out the horse's mouth first.'

'Christ! I'm not a horse.'

'Let me put it this way. If you were, I'd be interested enough at least to watch how you trot.'

'It's no wonder this country is full of old bachelors.'

'Let's step it out again,' said Maura, taking me by the hand.

As we shuffled around the floor some people watched me surreptitiously but everyone seemed friendly.

Then Maura nudged me. 'Look, he never misses an opportunity to be in the limelight.' The Fling Devlin was standing on the stage with the microphone in his hand. 'Wait till you hear this bullshit,' she said.

'Good people of Cambroestown,' began the Fling. 'I won't hold up proceedings, but before I say anything it would be remiss of me to ignore the little altercation of a few minutes earlier. However, I am hardly in a position to condemn such hijinks. Sure, in my younger days, didn't I get into a few fights myself.'

There was a tiny ripple of laughter.

'You would think that oul' cow would have run dry by now,' said Maura.

'Even though,' continued Fling, 'I am no longer active in the Cambroestown Dramatic Society due to my public service commitments, I want to congratulate the group on their continued success. Some years ago, I had the honour of having a role in that wonderful production of *Shadow of a Gunman*, whose themes I am of course personally familiar with.'

'Lord God, but he's one ignoramus,' whispered Maura. 'He thinks it was about IRA heroics.'

'What was it about?'

'Cowardice and deception, I would say.'

Not having seen the play I didn't comment. The politician continued to ramble on about the value of the arts for rural communities, and compared the Cambroestown productions favourably with Dublin's Abbey Theatre. He finally finished off by saying, 'I better not keep you back any longer. Just because my old legs are not what they once were, that doesn't mean I should be detaining you people from enjoying yourselves performing the dances of our forebears. Due to the sacrifices of earlier generations, we have in this Republic the hard-won privilege to so do. *Go raibh maith agaibh. Slán go fóill.*'

Fling waved his hand at the audience like an American presidential contender at a nomination convention and limped down the steps off the stage. Even though he spoke to everyone as he passed, people mostly seemed disinclined to enter into conversation with him. He made his way towards where we sat, reached out his hand to me in an excessive display of friendliness, and gushed to Maura, 'Hello Maura, introduce me to the man made good who has returned to claim his birthright.'

I shook his hand.

'Phillip Devlin TD, meet Josie Cambroe,' said Maura.

'You're very welcome back to the land of your people,' said the Fling. Before I could speak, he said, 'You know, some of my colleagues don't see new arrivals into their constituency as real people, only as possible votes come the next election. That was never my way. Maura will vouch for me when I say I know the people of Monaghan as well as I know my own family. In fact they are my family. Why, I remember Maura here when she was in the pram.'

'Don't embarrass me,' said Maura.

'You go back a long way,' I said.

The Fling nodded his head in agreement. 'Isn't that the truth. I have seen this country rise from the ashes and win the right to govern itself.'

I could have said you didn't win the fight to rule it all, but I had no intention of getting involved in Irish politics, even though it was Irish politics from an earlier age that had me here. Fling was about to say more when someone caught him by the elbow and asked if he could speak to him.

'Ah, the responsibility of office,' he said to me before shaking my hand again. 'We will have to have a longer chat soon.'

The Fling moved away, and I was about to say to Maura how interesting the night was turning out to be, when someone shouted from the door that there was a fire in the village. There was an immediate rush to the entrance. From the steps of the barn, smoke could be seen coming from somewhere. I reached the main street just as the fire brigade arrived with blue lights flashing.

It was my pub. Smoke billowed through the old rafters. A garda car pulled up and two gardaí took control of the situation, keeping the onlookers back. Like everyone else, I was not allowed near the conflagration. The firemen tackled the blaze. There wasn't anything I could do except stand there feeling helpless. I watched a fireman burst in the front door with an axe. Even standing well away I could feel a blast of heat escape from inside. A man aimed a hosepipe at the gaping hole and a gush of water came out. Suddenly it seemed I was on the front lawn of our home. My father was carrying me under his arm. He had his other arm around my mother. My feet were bare. My mother was screaming. The ground was covered in snow. We were all in our nightclothes. Masked men were roaring and shouting. Someone had hammered a crude sign into the ground. In big green letters it said, 'English Landlords Not Wanted.' A tall skinny guy was yelling and cursing and encouraging the others to burn the building to the ground.

Then Maura was shaking my arm, asking if I was all right.

'Do you see what they have done?' I said, pointing at the blazing pub.

'Yes. I see it.'

'Believe me, this time it's going to be different. This time no one's leaving.'

6

I was back again at the garda station, the usual hive of activity with lots of uniformed officers coming and going. After being told to wait, I sat on the same bench as the last time. The guy with the loud tie that I had seen in Donaghy's pub was also sitting there. I had plenty of time to appraise him. It wasn't just the tie that was different. He wore fawn trousers, shiny brown boots, a sports jacket and a trilby hat. He shook my hand and introduced himself as Peter Freeman, but he said everyone called him Podge. He was presently on bail and had to sign in at the station once a week. I didn't like to ask what he was charged with, but he volunteered the information.

'You can trust no one,' he said. 'I had been told that the road would be cleared but it was a trap. The customs had set up an ambush. A lorry load of cement lost.' He shook his head sorrowfully.

Obviously he was a smuggler.

'There have always been informers in this country,' he said. 'That's how every rebellion was lost. But our day will come.'

Also an IRA sympathiser, but he seemed to be a guy who would be good fun at a party.

I was taken into a room where Sergeant Love and Detective Dooley greeted me.

'Back already,' Love said.

I looked at the men again. Dooley was extremely thin with a long face. Even his lips were thin. I imagined a mouth that would open like a zip on a purse. Love had eyes sharp as a mouse. He was approaching middle age, and I couldn't decide if his grumpy persona was affected or real. Both policemen were facing me side by side.

The sergeant said, 'We need you to make a statement regarding the fire at your premises. But first, just to get a few facts straight that we didn't cover last time. You are an Australian, right?'

'I am Irish, but have lived in Australia for a long time.'

'Ah yes, that's correct, you're originally Irish.'

I didn't understand what being 'originally' Irish meant, but said nothing.

'As a matter of interest, how are you finding it living among us?'

'Fine.'

'The dampness isn't getting to you?'

'Not really.'

'So you might describe yourself as having settled in nicely.'

I took the last remark to be a statement and didn't respond.

'The fire occurred late at night, and you were attending the drama society's barn dance at the time,' said Love.

'Yes.'

Dooley took out a little leather wallet from his inside

pocket and withdrew the nail-file. He began working it around his fingernails. I wondered if the nail-file was some kind of comforter. If so, why did he need it? Surely asking me a few questions wouldn't cause him anxiety.

'Did anything untoward happen at the dance?' Dooley wanted to know.

I stared for a few seconds at the man's long skinny fingers and thought of the hand in the meadow.

'Not very much,' I said. 'The Crowley boys did a bit of playacting, nothing serious.'

'Nothing serious? It's said you beat up the three of them on your own.'

'I wouldn't call it beating them up.'

Dooley examined the back of his hand, the fingers spread wide. Why had he such an interest in his hand?

The sergeant continued the questioning. 'Are you some kind of John Wayne cowboy who can dispose of three attackers and describe it as nothing serious?' Love's lips shaped themselves into a kind of smirk. 'There's plenty of cowboys around here. Isn't that correct, Detective Dooley?'

'Without a doubt, Sergeant.'

'Don't they have real cowboys in Australia?' asked Love.

'I am prepared to make a statement regarding the fire,' I said. 'I expect you people to investigate how it happened.'

Love didn't react other than to train his sharp little eyes on me. 'Be assured,' he said, 'we will investigate all aspects of it.' He paused for a few seconds, and then said, 'Detective Dooley, take down a written statement from Mr Cambroe and get him to sign it.'

My statement was brief. I outlined how I checked the site

just before the workmen quit for the evening and everything was normal. I only knew of the fire the same time as everyone else.

Then Dooley asked me a strange question. 'Did you leave the dance at any time?'

'No.'

'So you were with Maura all evening?'

I assured him that was case.

Love had been leafing through a folder. He looked up and said, 'Have you romantic designs on the Glunt's daughter?'

'Who the hell is the Glunt?'

Love looked at Dooley. 'Maura Creighton's father. You said you were at the barn dance with her.'

'With respect, Sergeant, I don't think my romantic life is any of your concern, or has anything to do with your enquiries about who started the fire.'

Love stared at me for a few seconds. 'Let me explain something to you, Mr Cambroe. This is Monaghan. When a garda makes enquiries relating to a suspected crime they talk to all the individuals involved. I don't know how police forces operate in Australia, but here we like to know *everything* about those individuals, and that includes what brand of toothpaste they use, if any, *and* their romantic life. As a rule, all of this information is common knowledge, including the toothpaste, but in your case there is a dark cloud regarding what people know about you. So as the old saying goes, when in Monaghan do it the Monaghan way. In other words, don't keep any secrets from us.'

He was giving me a dressing down, and since I'd already

given my statement I stood up to leave. 'Everyone has secrets, Sergeant. Even in Monaghan.'

Neither man replied to this. I asked Love if he had any suspicions as to how the fire started.

'Just get in touch with your insurance company,' he said. 'We'll let you know if there are any developments.'

I waited for a couple of weeks but the gardaí didn't contact me, and I got very little information from the insurance company. It could have been started by a cigarette butt thrown carelessly by someone. Perhaps it had been smouldering for hours. Or maybe a drunk sleeping rough was responsible, and there were at least a couple in the area. I went over the night in detail with Maura.

She said she thought Soapie was still at the dance when the alarm sounded but she couldn't be sure. She was almost certain the older of the two brothers had left before the Fling arrived. If Soapie hadn't left, it was unlikely he started the fire unless he got someone to do it for him. Maura believed the fire was accidental, that none of the Crowleys would go to that extreme.

Jack, who had time on his hands and called regularly to see me, thought it was malicious. I told him about Love's rant concerning how little he knew about me and about him asking about my love life.

Jack laughed. 'Listen, Josie, this is Monaghan.'

'Oh God, no,' I said. 'You're not going to make the same speech?'

'Everyone here is supposed to know everything about everyone else.'

'It seems to be very important that it should be so,' I said.

Jack took a swallow of coffee, twitched his head like a bird a couple of times and became more reflective. 'Actually it's not that simple. Loads of secrets are hidden behind closed doors. It would be truer to say everyone *wants* to know everyone else's business. We Irish are famous for our friendliness to strangers, but that's not about sociability.'

'What is it about?'

'Nosiness. That's what masquerades as Ireland of the welcomes.'

'You're too cynical,' I said.

'Not everything is on the surface, Josie.'

'Maura said the same thing to me, so give me an example, Dr Freud.'

'You may smirk, but when he called Maura "the Glunt's daughter", he was taunting you about how little you know about her. You're not even familiar with the family nickname.'

'What's so important about that?'

'He knows all about her.'

'And?'

'My God but you're thick,' Jack said shaking his head. 'Love didn't tell you his real interest in your romantic life. He didn't tell you he and Maura are romantically linked.'

'What?'

Jack smiled, 'You're one slow learner. It's an open secret that he's been seeing her.'

For the second time that night I got up and made coffee. Maura and Sergeant Love! I found it hard to believe. He was much older than her. Why didn't she tell me? She told me about Mickey and Kevin, but not the sergeant. Did that mean she had more interest or less interest in him? I sat down at the table in my dressing-gown. The more I didn't sleep the more coffee I drank, and the more coffee I drank the more I couldn't sleep. The bay window was slightly ajar and a soft breeze entered the room. I went over to it, mug in hand, and looked out at the curved driveway. This would never do. I was forgetting my reasons for coming home.

Early the next morning I was at the pub where work was due to recommence. Only the foreman Pavee and his brother Simon were present. 'Where's everybody?' I said.

Pavee shook his head. 'You have powerful enemies, Mr Cambroe. We cannot get men to work on this site, and even if we did, it would be against our own interests to do the job. I am sorry.'

'Where am I at then?'

Pavee lifted a piece of burned rafter and flung it into a pile of rubble. 'I don't know. It's a huge job. Maybe others will do the work but it will be difficult for you. We just wanted you to know we have no personal animosity towards you and wish you good luck.'

The men got into their van and left me standing amidst the ruins, like a captain on the bridge of a sinking ship abandoned by its crew. No one was going to mourn the demise of this particular vessel. The village was deathly quiet. Where was everyone? I picked my way out of the forlorn site and stamped ash onto the pavement. It was only then I noticed a car parked a little way up the street, a big blue Ford Zephyr with a man sitting in it. He blew the horn at me, indicating he wanted me to approach. It was Podge with the loud tie.

'Hop in,' he said.

I couldn't think of anything else to do so I sat in beside him.

'You're in a spot of bother,' he said.

'You must be a mind reader.'

He laughed loudly. 'I like it, I like it.'

'It's not really funny,' I said.

'I know you're being boycotted.'

'Really?' I said, looking at the burnt out pub. 'How could you tell?'

'Gossip. This is Monaghan.'

I closed my eyes and drew a deep breath. 'If I hear that explanation for something one more time, I will choke the man who gives it.'

Podge laughed again. 'Do you want a gang of men to do the job?'

'That's a silly question.'

'Right then. I'll pick you up at six.'

Later that evening, Podge was getting his sunglasses to sit comfortably on his nose while he explained to me why he drove the car he did. 'It can often be a case of fur coat and no knickers,' he said. 'In my game, it's important to make an impression. If I sat in an Austin 35 and went about dressed like other people I wouldn't get the same attention, and when you're a wheeler-dealer like me, people need to take notice. They need to think this guy has the readies. But like I said, it can be a cover up.'

'At least you're honest about it.'

'That's only because I'm not trying to impress you, or do a deal with you.'

I looked out the window. We were travelling north towards South Armagh. The road was narrow and twisty. Then Podge slowed down, stopped the car and got out. He motioned me to do the same. 'Do you see that pebble on the road?' he said, pointing at a little stone about three yards ahead.

I nodded.

'See if you can spit that far.'

I looked at him. He was in earnest. 'Just do it,' he said.

I gave my head a shake. 'Stand back.' I pulled my head back and then spat as far as I could, easily clearing the pebble. Podge looked at me, nodded, and got back in the car. 'Get in,' he said.

We took off again. 'What was all that about?' I asked.

'I wanted to show you how daft it is.'

'What?'

'The border. You were able to stand in one country and spit all the way into another.'

'There was no marker to say that.'

'That's what the IRA argue. It's just a line on a map.'

'What's the story with them?'

'They abandoned their most recent campaign. Hopefully they're only taking a breather.'

'You're a supporter.'

'Of course I am.'

'But then there'll be no border to smuggle goods across. That's a contradiction for you.'

'Listen, my Australian friend. Ireland is full of

contradictions.'

As we travelled, the landscape changed from fields with shallow slopes to more hilly country. 'That's Slieve Gullion,' said Podge, pointing at a huge mountain ahead. 'It was volcanic once and the lava it spewed created all these hills around us.'

'If there's ever a united Ireland you can get a job as a travel guide,' I said.

Podge grunted something in reply, and then said, 'We're almost there.'

He pulled into a GAA pitch where about twenty young fellows were playing football.

'Are they training?'

'Not really,' Podge said. 'Playing football in the evening is what young people do in this part of the country. There's not much else. If I was ten years younger I'd be out among them.' Then he thought again. 'Although ten years ago I hadn't time to be playing football.' He took off the shades. 'Money and girls were my downfall.'

'I get the impression you haven't changed much.'

Podge looked at me. 'Does anyone ever really change? Have you changed?'

'I have.'

'Maybe, but only you know it. What the man from Australia was like before he came here is a mystery to people.'

'Believe me, I have changed.'

'In what way?'

'Are we going to sit here all night?' I said.

Podge got out of the car and called over one of the

footballers. I could see them having an animated discussion, and then the two of them came to me.

We were introduced. Jim Culhane was the fellow's name. Podge said he would put a gang of men together who would do the job if we could agree a price. I said if it was within reason we wouldn't fall out over it, and so it was settled. They would give me a price and start work the following week.

I knew I should be cooking for myself but instead decided that I deserved to have my lunch made for me. The most convenient place was the Monaghan Arms were Maura worked. As soon as I entered the lobby I saw that it was Mickey at reception. She must be on a day off. All of a sudden I wished I had made my own lunch. The dining room was full of people. Many took notice of me, but none spoke or acknowledged my presence. I wouldn't be known personally to any of them. The girl taking my order was professional and courteous. Maybe I was being paranoid in thinking I was being treated like a pariah.

As I finished my lunch, Mickey came over. He greeted me effusively. 'Hello my friend from long ago.'

I told him about the workmen not turning up and was no longer surprised that he already knew about it. 'I guess news travels fast in this town,' I said. 'Is Maura off today?'

'Yeah, but the good news is you will need lunch again tomorrow, and she will be on duty then.'

'Mickey, you're a nosy parker.'

He laughed and said, 'You're in Monaghan.'

'Yeah, yeah. Did you ever go abroad?'

He shook his head.

'Tour Ireland?' I asked. 'Go to Dublin?'

'People usually get to go to Dublin when Monaghan reaches a semi-final in the football championship, or when they are on their honeymoon, so I don't think I will be in Dublin anytime soon.'

I was happy he didn't feel too concerned whether he travelled or not.

The next morning I had a phone call from Jimmy Culhane. He was on site and all set to go, but was having trouble getting building supplies. The local suppliers said they were out of basic materials such as blocks, sand and cement. There were other places he could go for supplies, but it was time consuming and would cost more because of the distance to deliver.

I told Jimmy to keep the men on site. Enough was enough.

I walked into the hardware shop in the builder's yard and asked to see the manager. The couple of customers at the counter looked at me curiously, but by now I was used to the attention. It took quite a while for someone to appear. A small, thin man with a bald head came out from behind a partition. When he spoke it was with a slight stutter.

'What can I do for you, sir?' he managed to articulate.

'Can we speak privately?'

The little man rubbed his hand over his bald head as if he were patting down his hair, and seemed unsure what to do or say. 'Come into my office,' he said.

I followed him in and waited for him to close the door.

'What the hell is going on?' I said.

'Please explain, sir,' he stuttered.

'My builders have been told a yarn about blocks, cement and sand being in short supply.'

'Where have you the site?'

'You know damn well where I have the site. Let me explain something to you.' I put my hand in my pocket and drew out a handful of five pound notes. 'This is my money. It is as good as anyone else's, and it's cash on delivery. Now do I have to take my business elsewhere or will you be able to supply my needs?'

I could see the little man's dilemma. Even though someone had put pressure on him, he was trying to run a business in tough times. Turning down a cash customer was not easy. He looked again at the money in my hands. 'Let me see what the problem is. Wait here.'

He left the room but was back again very soon. 'That's sorted now,' he said. 'A huge building site on the other side of Monaghan cleared all our stock yesterday, but we have a delivery due in after lunch and we will gladly fulfil your order, Mr Cambroe.' I hadn't told him my name. On the way out I noticed that at the bottom of the yard, almost out of sight, were maybe thirty wooden pallets piled high with blocks.

A few days later I rang Jack and asked him to meet me for dinner in the Monaghan Arms. Maura was at the reception desk, and we chatted about the progress of the pub. I asked if she had any quiz questions for me. She thought for a minute. 'What do you call a bull sleeping in a field?'

I tried to think of the answer and was about to give up,

but then Jack came into the hotel. He greeted us both warmly, and he and I went into the lounge.

'You have your work cut out there,' he said as we sat down.

'What do you mean?'

'Maura.'

'What about her?'

'You fancy her.'

'You're imagining things.'

'I hope so, because you're well behind on the scoreboard, and as Michael O'Hehir our famous football broadcaster would say, time is ticking away.'

'Just supposing you're right, how come I'm so far behind?'

'Because Maura is one of the most sought after lassies around. Every bachelor in the locality is after her, and not just because of herself. She will also come into twenty acres of nice land.'

'If I *was* interested in her, it wouldn't be because of the land.'

'But it doesn't matter because you have no interest in her.'

'That's right.'

'What are you having to eat?' said Jack looking at the menu.

'I always have steak.'

'I'll have a mixed grill,' Jack told the waitress.

There were only a few people eating, mostly single men, probably travelling salesmen booked in for the night.

'Wouldn't it be great,' said Jack, 'if you had Maura to cook your dinner every evening.'

'I'm not thinking of Maura.'

'Oh, what are you thinking of?'

'I'm thinking of the work on the pub.'

'I heard you had trouble getting men and materials.'

'Yeah. Fill me in on what was going on.'

'The local contractors are all cousins and married into the Crowleys, so it's easy to understand where the pressure was coming from there. Finnegan's reluctance to supply materials is more intriguing.'

'Why so?'

'You would imagine he would only be delighted to do business.'

The waitress arrived with our order. 'I'm sure you have a theory?' I said.

Jack shook salt over his mixed grill. 'Yes, I have a theory.'

'Spit it out.'

'The Fling. His daughter is married to Finnegan.'

'Why would the Fling get involved?'

'You tell me.'

'I don't know.'

'I'm going to order tea. Do you want a cup?' said Jack.

'Coffee,' I said.

Jack gave the waitress the order and continued eating his mixed grill. 'Jesus, is this supposed to be steak? It's more like boot leather.'

'Don't complain,' I said. 'You're lucky to be getting steak in a mixed grill.'

Jack laughed. 'If it looks like steak and tastes like steak, it must be steak, but I am still not convinced.'

'That's just a suspicious mind manifesting itself.'

'My suspicious mind also tells me there's an issue between the Fling and yourself.'

'Just as a matter of interest, supposing I *was* interested in Maura, what would I do?'

Jack let his knife and fork fall onto his plate. 'God almighty, you're impossible.'

'What do you mean?'

'We were on a completely different subject, and now you jump to enquiring how you might go about courting Maura after maintaining you have no interest in her.'

'I don't. Reach me those tooth picks.'

'You're mooning over her like a calf that lost its mother. All I can suggest is you take her to a football match or to a dance at one of the local carnivals. Not that that would be very exciting for her.'

I left Jack outside the hotel door and then slipped back in. Maura was dealing with a guest at reception, so I read a newspaper that was lying on a chair. It was the local rag with pictures of the Fling and others at some recent party function. Mickey Patton was also in one of them with his good arm around the Fling's shoulder. It carried Fling's speech. In the little bit of it that I read, he was still lauding his part in Ireland's fight for independence. When Maura was free, I threw the paper aside and went up to her.

'Well, how was the steak?' she asked.

'One of these days I am going to have something else.'

'We'll see. People don't change easily.'

'I do.'

'What have you changed about yourself these past ten

years?'

'It would take too long to tell you. I was wondering if you'd like to go to Dublin for the day?'

Maura had been fiddling with a fountain pen. She dropped it on the desk and looked at me with her mouth half open. I'd never seen her so attractive.

After a few seconds, she said, 'Where did that come from?'

'We could go on the train, visit the zoo and see the sights,' I said.

She stood there not speaking, and then said, 'Let me think about it.'

'What's there to think about?'

'You wouldn't understand.'

'Try me.'

'I'll ring you and let you know.'

'Soon?'

'Yes,' she said.

'By the way, what's the answer to the question about the sleeping bull?'

'A bulldozer.'

I loved the way she laughed.

One week later we got a bus to Dundalk where we caught a train to Dublin. It was a glorious autumn day. At one point, as we chugged and rattled our way out of Dundalk station, Maura's face was framed in the glass window against a field of golden corn. I sat and watched not wanting the scene to change. We stopped in Dunleer and then passed over the viaduct at Drogheda. Other passengers in our carriage threw coins out of the window to the river far below and made a wish. At a tiny station just beside Mosney holiday camp, crowds of excited children and their parents got off to visit the resort for a day's outing. Maura and I spoke very little during the journey. She was taken in by the ever changing vista, and I enjoyed her interest in seeing the landscape from a new perspective. She had only been to Dublin twice before, both times by car. We got off at Amiens Street station and walked the whole way to Dublin Zoo in the Phoenix Park. Maura insisted on walking in order to see everything. It took us an hour but we got a feel for the city.

Dublin was different to Monaghan. People seemed more sophisticated and more businesslike. On reaching the zoo we had lunch, and afterwards we went to see the animals. Maura was spellbound by the monkeys. I stood back and watched the wonder in her eyes. Why was I enjoying that so much?

Later we went to O'Connell Street and climbed the steps inside Nelson's Pillar to the viewing platform at the summit.

'If I ever have children or grandchildren,' said Maura, 'I want to take them here and tell them I climbed this same monument long before they were born.'

Maura was fascinated by how small people were down below. She insisted she could see Monaghan, and then tried to catch one of the seagulls that hovered around the edifice. Others on the viewing platform gave her strange looks but she was oblivious. Afterwards we went to the Gresham Hotel for afternoon tea. A doorman dressed in some kind of strange uniform stood outside the huge front doors. When we entered, Maura gazed at the opulence of the foyer.

The walls were covered in expensive panelling. Priceless looking portraits and paintings hung on the polished wood. A magnificent crystal chandelier sparkled and glinted like sunlight off a lake on a summer day.

'I will have to get a job here,' said Maura.

'They couldn't afford you,' I said.

Tea was served in a silver-plated teapot with matching utensils. Maura was especially interested in the little sieve for placing on the cup to catch the tealeaves. She said her father loved to eat the leaves left in the cup, and wondered how a fortune teller could read a cup that had no tealeaves. The rich fruitcake reminded her of Christmas. Maura said the most striking thing was the fawning of the hotel staff. We were addressed by the waiters as 'Madam' and 'Sir'.

'Those who can afford to be here expect to be treated with undue deference,' I said.

'We are here, and don't expect special attention.' She put a tiny bit of icing into her mouth and rolled her eyes to heaven at the exquisite taste.

'That's one of the reasons people pay the huge prices.'

'They must be insecure.'

I laughed. 'Not everyone can be born and bred in Monaghan.'

Later we walked up Grafton Street. Maura marvelled at the fashion in the shop windows. One dress was priced at £19, and she said no dress on earth could be worth that. We walked around St Stephen's Green Park, which had on its autumn attire. Rust coloured leaves fell on little lakes where adults and children alike threw pieces of bread to eager ducks. Teenage boys and girls carried books under their arms and held hands as they strolled. Now and then a determined businessman carrying a briefcase would hurry past.

All too soon it was time to catch the last train home. By now Maura had stopped commenting on everything. Maybe her brain was processing all the information. We got back on the railway carriage. With the sound of steel wheels rumbling along steel tracks, she dropped off to sleep with her head resting on my shoulder. I gazed at her face. Black hair was brushed back from her forehead and tied in a ponytail with a red ribbon. Full rosy lips needed no enhancement by artificial means, and her pointed little jaw had just the hint of a dimple. Her mouth was closed, but I knew that when she smiled people felt that tiny bit better. It entered my head that maybe it was only me who thought so. This was followed by another thought. If that was true, and only I felt better when she smiled, did that mean she was something special to me. I rubbed my brow vigorously with two fingers. There was only one logical thing I could do.

I drove her home and stopped my car outside her house. She turned to me and said she wanted to thank me for a wonderful day. I took her in my arms, but when I attempted to kiss her she turned away.

'What's wrong?' I said, and tried to make a joke. 'Do people not kiss each other in Monaghan?'

She shook her head and gazed out of the side window. 'You don't understand.'

'What don't I understand?'

She brushed a mark on the glass but didn't say anything.

'Turn around. Look at me.'

Maura turned her head and looked me in the eye.

'Will you marry me?' I said.

I might as well have said the sky was about to fall. She dropped her head, closed one fist and clasped it to her chest. 'Oh my God,' she murmured.

There was silence for a minute, then she turned the door handle and jumped out of the car saying, 'I'm sorry, I'm sorry.'

She banged the door shut and ran up to her front door, fumbling for the keys in her handbag. I watched her disappear into the house. What did I not understand?

7

Another sleepless night. At eight o'clock in the morning the front door-knocker banged. When I answered, Sergeant Love was standing there rigged out in full uniform complete with peaked cap. Alongside him, Detective Dooley was dressed in plain clothes.

'Sorry to get you out of bed,' said Love. 'Can we have a few minutes of your time?'

He wasn't a bit sorry. The timing of their call was deliberate. I invited them in.

'Did you have a late night last night?' he said.

I tightened the belt of my dressing grown. He was baiting me, but I wasn't going to bite.

'Tea or coffee, gents?'

'No, we're fine,' said Dooley.

'Oh, well I must have my morning coffee. Rest there a minute.'

I went into the kitchen and let them wait while I made the coffee. 'You sure you won't have some?' I said, coming back into the sitting room.

'We're sure,' said Love.

I deliberately looked at my watch. 'Could this not have waited?'

'I thought Australians rose early.'

He was at it again. 'I'm not Australian.'

Dooley said, 'Mr. Cambroe, these are of course only routine enquiries. Can you tell us your movements on the night of March twelfth of this year?'

'Pardon me?'

Love lifted his eyes to the ceiling and told Dooley to repeat the question.

'Can you remember where you were and what you were doing on the night of March twelfth?'

'That's six months ago. How would I remember that far back? I was most likely working at rebuilding the bar.'

Love butted in. 'Then you will have witnesses to substantiate your claim?'

'Tell me what this is about.'

'Were you in Dublin recently?'

I glanced at him. Did he know Maura and I were in Dublin yesterday?

'I am not answering any more questions until you tell me what's going on.'

Dooley said, 'Do you remember the human hand that you discovered while out walking?'

'Of course I do.'

'It has come to light that it belonged to a Dublin prostitute.'

'Is she dead?'

'Oh, she's dead all right,' said Love with a smirk on his face. 'Forensic people have matched the tissue.'

'Was she killed in Cambroestown?'

'We don't know for sure,' Dooley said. 'Her body was

recovered from the River Liffey, but that doesn't mean she was killed in Dublin. Her normal beat was in Kildare Street and Merrion Square.'

'A high class location,' said Love. 'Right next to the Dáil.'

'The what?'

He shook his head again. 'The Irish parliament, where our elected TDs do their thing.'

'Is it only now they've discovered who the hand belonged to?'

'Yes,' said Dooley. 'The Dublin lads had a body with a missing hand, but who would have imagined it turning up in Cambroestown. It took a while for the two to be connected.' He took out his nail-file and began scraping under his fingernails. He was at the hand again.

'Do you live alone, Mr Cambroe?'

'You've asked me that before.'

'Do you ever feel lonely or in need of company?' said Love.

'Do you?'

'It's our job to ask the questions,' said the sergeant.

'You put me out of bed to ask me if I feel lonely?'

'Mr Cambroe,' said Dooley, 'we have a hard job to do so your cooperation would be very much appreciated.'

'What have I got to do with the murder of a prostitute on the streets of Dublin?'

'Most likely nothing,' said Dooley, concentrating on his nails.

'Mr Cambroe,' said Love, 'you haven't been here a wet day and there's been a human hand found on your property, you have been involved in fights at a local barn dance, you have your business premises destroyed by fire, perhaps intentionally. We know practically nothing about your background. Now we discover the hand belongs to a murdered Dublin whore. Need I go on?'

I was stuck for what to say. In spite of the sergeant's little speech, I thought his visit might have more to do with my interest in Maura than a murder investigation. I wondered if he was following me and knew we had been in Dublin, or had she rang him and told him about it. I got up and walked over to the window. The foliage on the trees at the front of the house had only now begun to change colour. The seasons turned later in Monaghan than Dublin. I was five years old when myself and Mickey Patton had climbed high in the branches trying to reach a crow's nest. Mickey got stuck between two branches and I had to call my father to rescue him. He was angry at us for being up there in the first place. My mother chided him. She said children climb trees to reach the top. It was a natural instinct to be king of the world and was at the root of all civilisation. Father just grunted and said that in this instance civilisation got stuck in the branches.

'Are you with us, Mr Cambroe?' said Love

Now both of my parents were buried far away from here in a foreign land, a land they had been forced to flee to. Those responsible had to be held to account. I turned back and faced the two policemen. Dooley fiddled with the nail-file. Love leaned back in the armchair with his legs folded and his cap placed on one knee.

'I don't know for sure,' I said, 'but I was probably here at home.'

'If you were at home could anyone verify that?' said Dooley.

'No.'

'What about Maura the hotel receptionist?'

'What about her?'

'Could she give you an alibi?'

'Alibi is a strong word,' I said. 'It suggests something more than just routine enquiries.'

'Most cases,' said Love, 'are solved by eliminating . . . I won't use the word suspects, just in case you think it too strong a word. But if we know you were here on the night the unfortunate lady was murdered then you could hardly have done it, and so we move on elsewhere.'

It was the tone of his voice that annoyed me more than anything. 'I wonder, Sergeant, if you have anyone to corroborate where you were on March twelfth or thirteenth or any other random date you care to mention?'

'There's no need to be aggressive, Mr Cambroe. We are just public servants doing our job.'

'You are not acting like servants, and I would rather you do your job elsewhere.'

'If you have nothing to hide, why are you getting angry?' said Love.

'I'm not angry, but I am pissed off at your implied accusations that I had something to do with the murder of a Dublin prostitute.'

'We are sorry if we have given that impression,' said Dooley, who had finally stopped fiddling with the nail-file. 'But we don't often find limbs belonging to Dublin prostitutes here in Cambroestown.'

Love stood up to leave. 'I had an old sergeant once,' he said, again in the same slightly threatening tone. 'He always said, "Follow what sticks out." Lord have mercy on his soul, but I have no doubt he would say that you, Mr Cambroe, stick out.'

I knew it was Maura's day off, so I phoned Jack and asked him to meet me in the hotel that evening. When he arrived he greeted me with, 'I don't know what we all did for gossip before you landed among us.'

'Somebody buried a prostitute's hand in the Big Meadow, and I don't think that had anything to do with me arriving in this little village of yours.'

Jack had his arm raised to try and attract the barman's attention. He let it drop like a stone. 'What? The hand belonged to a prostitute. Who was she? How do you know?'

Finally, a piece of news that hadn't been spread. 'There you go,' I said. 'Cambroestown and murdered prostitutes. What do you think?'

Jack twitched his head a couple of times. 'I think your belief that there's no connection between your arrival and the hand being found in your field could very well be wrong. Fill me in on this news.'

I told him all about the policemen calling, and he listened intently.

When I finished, he said, 'Is there anything else you should tell me?'

'There isn't much more to say, except that I asked Maura to marry me.'

I might as well have punched him in the stomach.

*

That evening I got a call from Maura. She wanted to meet me and said she would be out walking towards Shaw's Lough. If I came along I could pick her up. Clearly she didn't want us seen together.

She sat in silence as we drove out into the countryside past the lough and finally stopped the car beside one of the many more remote lakes dotted around the area. Each of them had their own charm. This one was almost entirely surrounded by thick foliage and had a little island in the middle with fuchsia plants still in full bloom dotted here and there. The water was calm as a sheet of ice.

'It's so peaceful and beautiful,' said Maura, gazing out of the windscreen.

I looked at her and nodded. I knew she wore no makeup, and wondered if there were any cosmetics on the market that could make a face more beautiful.

'Fuchsia is my all-time favourite,' she said.

'Why?'

'It grows wild and free everywhere and you have its beautiful bells all year from spring to autumn. Once I get my own garden I am going to have them everywhere and make jam from the berries.'

I looked out across the lake at the island. Even from this distance I could see bees encouraged by the Indian summer buzzing around the blossoms.

'From now on,' I said, 'every time I see a fuchsia bush I will think of you, and how lovely you looked at this moment.'

'I would love it if you did.'

'I will. I promise.'

'No matter what happens?'

'No matter what happens.'

Maura kept her face away from me. 'It's better not to know the future.'

'You sound sad,' I said.

She stayed silent for a few moments.

'John Love has asked me to marry him.'

It was my turn to be silent. Then I said, 'So have I.'

Maura put her two hands over her face. 'You don't understand,' she said into them.

'So you keep telling me.' I tried to put my arm around her shoulder, but she drew away. 'You owe it to me to tell me what I don't understand.'

She took her hands from her face and blurted out, 'It's the land. If I married you, you would be the owner of the land or at least it would be in your name.'

'Listen,' I said, 'I am not in any way interested in your fields. You can sell them and keep the money for all I care. It's you I want, not the land.'

'That's what you don't understand. The land goes with me. Whoever I marry, that's the name that will be on the deeds. I told my father about you, even though I already knew the response. He said no man from the big house would ever get his hands on Creighton land. The land belongs to me and must be kept in the family.' She paused before saying, 'I am the only child and can't go against my father's wishes.'

Just then a grey heron swooped out of the sky and landed at the edge of the lake on long thin legs. We watched it parade proudly around in the stillness for a couple of seconds.

'What's wrong with my name?' I said.

'There are still people in Cambroestown who hate what they perceive to be the gentry. Even though you are not really the gentry, you bear the Cambroe name.'

'And that silly thing means you can't marry me.'

'It's not silly to my father. That's what you don't understand.'

Every so often the heron would stick its long curved beak under the water. I wondered if it had a mate. 'Why Love?' I said.

'He is a kind man who I know will be good to me, and I can be sure he is not marrying me because of the farm.'

'Jesus,' I muttered under my breath. 'Twenty lousy acres. They're hardly worth talking about.'

'I know how strange it might seem to you that a little bit of land can be so significant, but my father is old stock. He is a fair, upright man, and for that reason he won't let go of the things that he was taught were important.'

Again there was silence in the car. Then Maura said, 'I would love to have a little house out on that island. I could catch fish in the lake and be away from the world with only herons for company.'

I had one hand on the steering wheel. Maura reached over and covered it with her own. 'I'm sorry,' she said. 'I'm hurting as much as you, but this is our way. Nothing can change it. If my father were to die tonight, I would still have to abide by his wishes.'

She leaned over and gave me a peck on the cheek. 'I love

you,' she whispered. Then she said, 'Take me home.'

Jack expressed no surprise when I told him what had happened. 'You have to appreciate the value set on even a small piece of land,' he said. 'At one time those few acres could mean, no *would* mean the difference between dying and surviving, so their symbolic worth outstrips all other considerations for older generations.'

'Is there nothing to be done?'

'If you marry Maura she becomes Mrs Cambroe, so the land now belongs to the name Cambroe.'

'It's just a name,' I said.

'Your family was burned out and forced to flee because of that name.'

That night in bed while I was agonising over Maura, Jack's words came back to me. He was right. We were burned out and forced to flee. I would have to get myself back on track.

8

For the next few weeks I busied myself in helping Culhane with the bar renovations. I'd arrive on the site at seven and be the last to leave. Culhane said I was as good as two men. He didn't know that I was doing it to exhaust myself so I might get a few hours' sleep.

After two months of work we were finally set for the opening night. The side-bar hadn't quite been finished, but it wouldn't be needed yet. I added little Australian touches around the lounge: pictures of kangaroos, a few authentic boomerangs, and an aboriginal didgeridoo hanging from the ceiling behind the bar. Sawdust on the flagged floor added a rustic element, and instead of Men and Ladies or *Fir* and *Mná* on the toilet doors, I had printed Joey and Sheila.

I employed two barmen for the big opening and booked the Country Cowboys.

'I guess you know what to play to suit the crowd,' I said to Mark, the band leader.

Mark wore a shiny red showband shirt, and had a black cowboy hat hanging on one of the microphones. 'We can only play what we know, but have no worries. The punters who come here will want Irish ballads, country and western, and rebel songs. There won't be any demand for Mozart or

Beethoven.'

'You think anyone will come?' I said.

'They come everywhere else we play,' said Mark, testing the chords on his guitar.

I chatted to the barmen and asked them if they wanted to have a sandwich in the kitchen before it got busy. Maurice said he would go first and then Jim could go. I told Jim about my experience of working bars in Australia. Sometimes it was the only kind of work I could get. Maybe the big difference between there and here was in the way the pint of Guinness was pulled. Only in Ireland was the pouring of a pint seen as an art form requiring special tuition. Jim said he always wanted to go to Australia. In my case I didn't have an option, but I kept that to myself. He'd have no interest in ancient history.

At the drummer's tap on the side of his drum the band broke into a full melody of music, and then just as abruptly stopped again. They did this a few times before I guessed they were rehearsing new material.

Maurice returned shortly. He said the crowd would soon be coming in, that people were strange, they would all arrive at the same time as if they were programmed by some invisible watch. I went outside to have a look around. Other than the few cars belonging to the band, the street was empty. Was it the same at Donaghy's up the street? I decided to take a look and meandered slowly up the footpath, hoping no one would see me checking on the opposition. There were a lot of vehicles parked outside Donaghy's, and the din coming from inside suggested there was a big crowd. I turned back, and was half way to the bar when a car sped by carrying a number of youths. It wheeled around and drove back towards me again. Just as it was going past, a youth shouted, 'Fuck off home you murderer.'

I watched as it sped down the road. When I got back, there were still no cars outside my place. Inside, the only customers were Mickey Patton and Podge. Then the workmen and their wives came in, and although they didn't say anything, their faces registered surprise at the absence of customers. I went into the kitchen. Maurice sat glumly at the table resting his chin on his hands.

He looked up when I entered. 'It's not looking good,' he said. 'People always come to an opening even if it's only for the free first drink.'

'Maybe it's still too early.'

Maurice shook his head.

I went out and told Jim to give drinks on the house to everyone, including the band. It was better to keep up an optimistic front even if I didn't feel it. The group on the stage kept on playing lively tunes. The door opened and everyone turned their heads to see Jack enter. I met him halfway and put out my hand to greet him. 'Welcome, my friend.'

He looked around him. 'You don't need friends just now, you need customers.'

'I guess there's a difference between the two.'

'Yes,' said Jack. 'But in your case it is irrelevant as, *prima facie,* you have neither.'

'Jim,' I said to the barman, 'give this legal eagle whatever he's having.'

Jack took a stool at the bar and I sat beside him. 'Are you

not taking something yourself?' he asked.

'No.'

'Alcohol,' said Jack, 'was invented for two purposes: to help you celebrate, and to help you feel sorry for yourself. It seems to me you tick both boxes tonight.'

'You think I don't know that,' I said. 'The only thing that keeps me dry is an ache in my stomach that no amount of alcohol will relieve. I came to Ireland to get rid of that ache and that's what I intend to do.'

'Everyone copes with disappointment in their own way,' said Jack. 'In Ireland the vast majority uses the same means.'

'For me that's not an option,' I said. 'But it is depressing there's no one here.'

'Why would they be here? One, they don't know you. Two, regardless of what the lawyers said about benevolent landlords in the big house, the truth is there has always been resentment to the occupants of the manor. Those negative perceptions stay in folk memory. Just think of old Creighton's attitude. And leaving all that aside, the Crowleys aren't too happy with you and they have a lot of connections in this area. Even the free drink is no inducement as Val up the street is doing a "chicken in the rough" all on the house.'

'So what can I do?'

'Hang around. In ten or fifteen years they might accept you.'

I didn't reply, and we sat listening to the music for some time while I kept my eye on the door. A few people came in wearing curious expressions. They got a free drink and left again as soon as they finished it. Only one bothered to come over and wish me good luck.

Then the bar door opened with a flourish. The Fling Devlin strode in with another man in tow, probably his driver. 'Hello, the house,' he bellowed walking towards us. 'I just called in to wish you luck on your new venture,' he said addressing me.

'Thank you.'

'I'm sorry I never got time to call with you and commiserate when you had the fire. You know what it's like, parliamentary business and affairs of state.'

'That's okay,' I said.

'I'm sure the fire was accidental. No one around here is cruel or evil enough to burn down a neighbour's business.'

The Fling looked around him, counting how many customers were in the bar. 'The drinks are on me,' he guffawed. 'I wouldn't want to take a slate off the roof.' He moved aside to have a word with Podge.

'What does the slate thing mean?' I asked Jack.

'An old saying. It's considered bad luck not to buy something if you are in a shop that's just been opened.'

The Fling forgot to include the band in his largesse, and didn't comment on the lack of customers. 'Unfortunately, I can't stay,' he said. 'I have two more meetings to attend tonight.'

He paid for the drinks, shook my hand again, saying, 'Good luck,' and swept his way out of the place.

'That guy would go to the opening of a grave if he thought he'd get a vote,' said Jack.

'He didn't hang around.'

'Yeah, he could be doing himself more harm than good by associating with people like you.'

The music stopped playing and Mark came over. He hadn't even bothered to put on the hat. 'There's nothing worse than playing to the walls,' he said.

'Most people have played to the walls in their time,' said Jack. 'Even Frank Sinatra went through lean times.'

'I'm not Frank Sinatra.'

'You're right about that,' Jack retorted

'You may as well finish up,' I told Mark. 'You will be paid anyway.'

I went over to the counter where the builders were preparing to leave. One of them asked if I intended on completing the side bar. I told him it was full steam ahead until the job was done. Then I told Maurice and Jim that on account of the poor turnout, I would cover the bar myself.

After everyone else had left, Jack said, 'At least you won't have any problem clearing the place.'

'I bet they all went straight to Donaghy's.'

'No doubt,' said Jack.

'If you're right about it taking years before I'm accepted, I've a serious problem.'

'Sometimes we just have to accept things.'

'Some things aren't easy to accept.' I rounded the bar, poured Jack a fresh pint and placed it before him. 'Maybe I should have told you all this before now, but this is not just a business enterprise.'

'No?'

'It's not easy to explain.'

'Try me.'

'When we were burned out and had to emigrate, although I was very young, I vowed that someday I would come back home, buy the old place and show them.'

'Show who what?'

'The people who chased us out of the country.'

'God almighty, Josie.'

'You're surprised at that?'

'They're probably all dead by now.'

'Maybe, maybe not,' I said.

'Are you looking for revenge?'

'Not revenge.'

'What then?'

'Justice.'

'Justice, you say. How do you get justice?'

'The Cambroe name is back in the family home. If this business is successful, it will go some way to show my family are still at the centre of life in this community.'

'You said, "some way". Does that mean you have other plans? What if you find out who done the burning?'

'I don't know yet. I will jump that ditch when I come to it.'

Jack didn't say anything for a few moments. Then, as if he had made up his mind about something, he looked at me and said, 'Perhaps I *do* know of the pain that can be involved in letting people down.' He swirled the beer around in his glass, studying the frothy liquid. 'I knew a young fellow one time who desperately wanted to be a barrister. He had the high-minded idealism that only belongs to the young, and fantasised about arguing for the downtrodden and the innocent. It wasn't easy, however after much effort and sacrifice he qualified. But things didn't work out the way he expected. As a newcomer, briefs were difficult to come by.

Those that he did get were not very fulfilling – debates about rights of way and such like. They were boring in the extreme for a young man who wanted to right the wrongs of the world.'

Jack took a drink and continued. 'He could have overcome all this, but then the girl that he was madly in love with met someone else. The young fellow was devastated and became depressed. He could hardly concentrate on anything. His spirits were so low, suicide entered his mind. Then another friend he had roomed with when in college, and who was now a solicitor, contacted him. This solicitor friend had been representing a youth charged with murder and wanted him to be his barrister at the trial. His friend told him that he thought the accused was innocent. This was the young fellow's big chance, what he always wanted to do. But he was going through an awful time over the girlfriend. At first he turned the case down. However, following a lot of persuading by the solicitor, he agreed to take it on. After the initial interview with the accused, he was convinced of the fellow's innocence, and came to the conclusion that the lad had psychological problems that weren't immediately evident. He told the accused not to worry and promised him he'd be found innocent.'

Jack took another long swallow of beer. 'But the young barrister wasn't able to give the case anything like the attention it needed. He was on anti-depressants, tranquilisers, sleeping tablets, waking tablets, you name it. Sometimes he was so drunk with medication he didn't know what he was at. The inevitable happened. He lost the case. The accused was sentenced to fifteen years for a crime he didn't commit. Just before he was led away, he looked at his barrister. It was a look the barrister would never forget.'

'And you never forgot it,' I said.

'No, I never forgot it. I lied to you in the courtroom that day that I just liked watching court cases.'

'What happened?'

'The young fellow got a different barrister and was acquitted on appeal, but he spent a lengthy time in prison before his case came up again. I ended up in a psychiatric hospital until I recovered. Then I moved to Cambroestown and got a job in an accountant's office. I could never go back to law after what I let happen.'

There was silence between us. Then Jack said, 'I never told that story to anyone before. But you aren't a much of a talker.'

Again there was silence.

Jack finished the last of his drink and said, 'It's time I was going home.'

I told him I'd give him a lift. My Land Rover was parked outside. As soon as I opened the bar door I saw that the wheels were flat and the tyres slashed.

We inspected the damage, most likely inflicted by a Stanley knife.

I told Jack about finding the dead dog on my porch and said, 'Who do *you* think is doing the harassing?'

'You will have to go back to the police and find out if they've made any headway, either on the hand or on the fire. Your house was burned when you were a child, and now when you come home a fire burns your business. There has to be a connection.'

*

Sergeant Love sat back in his chair and folded his arms as I was shown in to his office. He seemed annoyed to see me, and when I asked about the inquiries he leaned his forearms on the desk.

'Mr Cambroe, I have no idea how the police in Australia go about their business, but here in Ireland, operational matters relating to an ongoing investigation are not divulged to the general public.'

'I'm not the general public,' I said. 'I am the victim.'

Love leaned back in his chair again. 'Victim, as you describe yourself, or not, when you need to be informed of anything, that will be done.'

'I've the right to know how the investigations are going.'

'The right?' The policeman shook his head dismissively. 'We'll make sure your rights are protected.'

I was beating my head against a wall. 'Any progress on who started the fire?'

'Do you know how many business fires are started by the owner?' said Love.

I looked him in the eye. 'What are you suggesting?'

'I'm suggesting nothing, just asking a simple question.'

'I have no idea.'

Love took a sip from a mug of tea. A half-eaten biscuit sat on a plate beside it. 'The answer, Mr Cambroe, is a lot.'

'It's my fire that I'm concerned with.'

'Oh, be assured, Mr Cambroe, we will find out who caused your fire.'

It sounded to me like a threat.

9

I opened the pub each evening at five but had very few customers. Jack called for a pint and a chat most evenings. Podge and Mickey also stopped by occasionally. A few times individuals that had been barred in Donaghy's came in. If they weren't drunk, I served them. Just because they had dirtied their bib elsewhere didn't mean I had to refuse them. Invariably, however, they would be accepted back where they normally drank.

One evening two women came in. Jack addressed them by their names, Angel and Mary. Angel was approaching middle-age and looked the younger of the two. Thin with mousy blonde hair, she was dressed in tight jeans and a woollen sweater. She wore a lot of makeup and smelled of perfume. I guessed Mary was either a spinster or a widow. She had grey hair. A long overcoat concealed her other clothes. Her only concession to glamour was bright red lipstick and matching finger nails.

Angel asked me where the toilets were, and I pointed them out either side of the bandstand. Angel went into the men's toilet and Mary followed her to tell her of the mistake. When the older lady came back she explained that Angel suffered from dyslexia. Jack said it must be terrible to have that condition. Mary said she wouldn't order a drink until Angel returned.

After ten minutes Angel hadn't appeared, and I suggested to Mary that she go and check on her. Mary did so, and after a couple of minutes she came out of the toilet holding Angel by the arm.

'She couldn't find her way out,' said Mary, and then to Angel, 'You're going to have to go back to the specialist and get yourself checked again.'

'Why?'

'Because your dyslexia is getting worse.'

'Are we having a drink seeing as we are here now?' asked Angel.

'Why do you think we came?'

'How would I know why you're here. I'm getting a drink anyway, do you want one?'

Mary studied the bottles behind the bar. 'I don't know what to have.'

'Hurry up and make up your mind,' said Angel. 'I'm dying to go to the toilet. Mr barman, while she's deciding, give me a vodka and white.'

I said I would serve Mary, but I wouldn't serve Angel.

She forgot about the toilet and became very indignant, claiming I had no right to refuse her. She demanded a reason.

'I don't have to give a reason,' I said.

'You think I'm drunk,' she said. 'I haven't had a drink in days.'

'I can vouch for her,' said Mary. 'This is the first pub we visited today.'

'I'm sorry,' I said.

'You cannot insult me like this,' said Angel. 'I will report you.'

'Come on, let's go, Angel,' said Mary. 'It's no wonder nobody comes into this place.'

Angel settled herself on the high stool and said, 'No, I have my rights. I intend on staying here until I'm served. I am a respectable woman and will not be treated like a tramp.'

I moved from behind the bar and repeated, 'I'm sorry.'

Mary took Angel by the arm, 'Please, Angel, let's get out of this dump.'

Angel knew she had no option but to leave. Jack's empty glass was sitting on the counter. She lifted it and pointed it menacingly at me. 'I wouldn't think twice of cutting your throat.'

When she got off the seat, Mary grabbed the glass from Angel's hand. 'Leave him be,' she said. 'There's plenty of other places where they know how to treat decent people.'

She manoeuvred Angel towards the door. As the two women left, Angel shouted back at me, 'Go home to Australia where you come from.'

When the door closed, I said to Jack, 'Do you know them well?'

'Yes. Angel, her real name is Angela, has a reputation for being fond of drink. She has a long-suffering husband, but she's very popular with the men. Why did you not serve her?'

'She was in no fit state.'

'She had no drink on her as far as I could tell.'

'Maybe not.'

'Josie, I despair that you will ever build up custom here.'

A couple of evenings later, Jack was there again when Angel came in, dressed almost the same as the last time. She strode up to the bar and settled herself on a high stool. I said, 'Hello,' and Angel said, 'Hello,' back, and then, 'This place is very nice.'

'Thanks. What can I get you?'

After musing for a few moments, she asked for a vodka and white. I served the drink. Angel took a sip from the glass and then got off the seat saying, 'I love the décor. Do you mind if I take a look around?'

'Feel free.'

While she was inspecting the lounge, Jack, in low voice, said, 'She doesn't remember being here before. Why did you serve her this time?'

'The eyes,' I said.

'What do mean the eyes?'

'Did you ever hear of Korsakoff Syndrome?'

'No.'

'Did you ever hear of alcoholic blackouts?'

'Yeah.'

'The last time she was in here, she was in a blackout.'

'How do you know?' asked Jack.

'It was the vacant look in her eyes that I noticed first.'

'How do you know so much about all this?'

'Working behind the bar in some of the joints in Australia, you soon learn to know when someone is in a blackout.'

Jack thought for a moment. 'In my younger days, I had nights that are a blur to me.'

'That's slightly different, although I know doctors would

say it isn't. When someone is in an alcohol induced blackout, it's as if they're taking pictures with a camera with no film. They're snapping away as normal, but nothing is recorded.'

'It's like the old joke – I had such a great night I can't remember a thing.'

'Yeah, but if it becomes permanent, you have what's known as a wet brain.'

Angel came back to her seat. 'I want to wish you good luck. It's lovely.'

'Isn't it nice?' said Jack casually. 'Is this the first time you've been in?'

'Yeah, I have been meaning to call for some time, but you know how it is.'

'Jesus,' murmured Jack to himself.

Angel sipped from the glass. 'You will find it very difficult here,' she said to me. 'People are so narrow minded.'

'Do you reckon?'

'Believe me I know. They spread rumours about you.'

I shrugged my shoulders. 'Yeah, maybe.'

Angel finished her vodka and asked for the same again. 'I pay them no heed. They're all a bunch of gossips.'

'Folks can be cruel,' said Jack.

'You don't know the half of it. Some of the good Christian ladies around this place would even try to decide who should be allowed to go to mass and who shouldn't.'

I served the drink and said, 'Not too many people have wished me good luck. This one's on the house.'

Maura was constantly on my mind. I managed to stay away

from the hotel where she worked. Sometimes I told myself I should go there for dinner, though I knew in my heart it wasn't for dinner I'd be going. I contemplated ringing her to ask about something or other. But she would know it was just an excuse to talk to her, and so far I'd been able to resist.

Business didn't improve. Jack and Podge were my only regulars. I christened the pub the Phoenix Bar. A couple of homosexuals came in now and again because they knew they wouldn't be bothered by anyone. Others seeking seclusion sometimes drifted in, including a glamorous young female accompanied by a middle-aged gentleman, rumoured, according to Jack, to be a parish priest from across the border in the North of Ireland. The girl had a huge liking for Pernod and white lemonade, and a capacity for the stuff that was astounding. Her companion didn't drink much, his excuse being that he was driving. Jack didn't agree with Podge that the lady might be the priest's housekeeper. Podge said men of the cloth led lonely lives. Jack said loneliness wasn't this clergyman's real problem. He had another, maybe more expensive one.

Angel still came in on a regular basis and was always full of chat. I decided her blackout may have been a one-off following a particularly heavy bout of drinking. Jack had stopped boasting of his wild youth and the lost nights.

Angel took a great interest in trying to conjure up ideas that would help business. She seemed to be something of an eccentric who refused to let ordinary things rule her life. Perhaps she found being a housewife frustrating and needed other interests to give her a sense of satisfaction. But these interests it seemed always brought her to a pub, and for the moment mine was her local.

One of her suggestions involved having a quiz team that could compete against other pubs. A problem with this idea lay in the fact the each team required four members. Jack, Podge, Mickey and myself could make up a team, but the rules required eight names to be registered. A shortage of players also applied to having a darts team. I put in a pool table, and became very adept at the game myself as I had plenty of time to practice. I installed a poker machine, but had to get rid of it after a couple of months. A little old lady who lived locally got hooked on it. Probably out of loneliness she would come in to me for company, but very quickly became addicted to the machine. I couldn't bear to watch her sit there all evening feeding it her pension money.

I never worried about official closing time since there were so few customers, and sometimes Jack, Podge and myself would sit on chatting until well after midnight.

One night the three of us were talking in the bar when Sergeant Love arrived. He told me he was summonsing me for serving alcohol after hours. It was less than five minutes after official closing time. I explained that there was no intention of breaking any laws, that we were just chatting and I was about to lock up. A month later I got the summons. I employed a local solicitor to represent me in court. He told me to expect a small fine and that would be the end of the matter.

On the day of the court, the magistrate was clearly hungover. I watched as he sentenced a vagrant to a month in prison for being drunk and disorderly.

The vagrant shouted out, 'You should be putting yourself in jail for a month, Your Honour.'

'I'm increasing your sentence to two months,' said the judge.

'Why not make it three months?'

'Three months.'

'Make it six.'

'Six months.'

'Make it twelve.'

'Take him away,' said the dispenser of the law.

When my case came up my lawyer pleaded not guilty. However, the magistrate found me guilty and endorsed the pub licence. This was a harsh penalty. Three endorsements meant losing the licence, so just one more would leave me on the edge. I felt my lawyer should have been more assertive.

'I couldn't be,' he said.

'Why not?'

'Love is a garda sergeant.'

'So what?'

The lawyer shrugged his shoulders. 'There are some cases he doesn't want to lose.'

I asked Jack for his opinion on what had happened. He was a barrister after all.

'I *was* a barrister,' he reminded me. 'Love doesn't like you.'

'Tell me something I don't know.'

'Why are you surprised at the outcome of the case then? Love is a sergeant. The magistrate is a roaring alcoholic. Your lawyer has a big family and needs to win more important cases than yours.'

'What can I do about it?'

'You can appeal it to a higher court. But what's going to change between now and then? It sounds to me like a waste of money.'

Angel had been listening to us and she advised me not to lose heart. She knew of someone.

A week later she came into the bar with a dishevelled middle-aged geezer any barman would be wary of serving. She bought him a double whiskey and told me this was the person she had mentioned. His name was Peters and he was a barrister.

He looked like another drunk to me.

Angel's legal genius swallowed the large whiskey in one go and said, 'I needed that.' He focussed his gaze on me. 'We'll win hands down. First, the details. How much underage were the guys you served?'

Any faint hopes I had were dashed. The guy was a loony. 'It's not an underage case.'

'The excise people. How many bottles did they take away for sampling?'

'And it's not about drinks being watered down.'

'Angel, will you order another round and I'll sort you out later? What the hell *are* you charged with, Mr . . . whatever your name is?'

'Serving alcohol after hours.'

'What was the fine?'

'I got my licence endorsed.'

'Who was the magistrate?'

'Deery?'

'A drunken bastard. Tell your lawyer to appeal the case to the circuit court. You will require a barrister. That's me.'

'Let me explain what happened.'

'No need. By the way, I rushed out of the house without any money. Put my drinks on the tab in place of a retainer.'

When the case came around, I still hadn't heard from Peters since that first meeting. Angel said he sometimes met clients in pubs and hotels. This resulted in shorter office hours.

'He drinks too much,' I said. 'I think he has a problem.'

'Not at all,' said Angel. 'For God's sake, I down nearly as much myself, and I'm not much of a drinker.'

On the morning of the hearing, Jack and I met Love at the entrance to the courthouse.

'Good morning, Sergeant,' I said.

Love grunted something about it not being a good morning for long. The attendees in court were a different type than at the licensing assizes. The majority of them were young, some only teenagers. They huddled in little groups outside the building like sheep anticipating a storm. Many of them were smoking. Barristers in white wigs strutted around with documents under their arms. A number carried important looking briefcases. There were adults there also, mostly parents of those being tried. They seemed more concerned than their children. Two youths in handcuffs were taken from an armoured carrier by prison warders and hustled through a side door.

Inside, Peters sat in the well of the court. He was no better dressed than when he first appeared in the Phoenix. The barrister's colleagues seemed to be keeping their distance on the bench. Maybe there was a smell of drink off him.

The judge was the same judge who granted my bar licence. When the case was called, he looked over at me. His glasses rested on the tip of his nose. 'Ah, Mr Cambroe, I remember you. A very interesting case indeed.'

The clerk of the court read out the nature of the charge. Peters rose. 'Your Honour, it may save time if I'm allowed to address the court before proceedings begin.'

'This is somewhat unusual,' said the judge with an air of resignation. 'However, I am minded to accede to your appeal. It is seldom enough that we have the good fortune to benefit from learned counsel's noteworthy familiarity with the intricacies of law.'

Peters was on his feet again. 'I thank you, Your Honour, for granting my request, and for your most gracious words.'

He lifted a sheet of paper and held it high in the air. 'The relevant passage of law pertaining to the present case clearly states, *The holder of the said licence shall not have it endorsed on a first offence.* Your Honour, this was my client's first offence. The manner in which justice has been administered in this instance is demonstrably flawed.'

Peters sat down. The judge looked at the prosecuting superintendent. The superintendent stood up. 'Your Honour, my function is to supply evidence, as happened during this case in the lower courts. It is the presiding officer's role to decide guilt or innocence, and to impose whatever sentence he decides is pertinent. If there is maladministration at this point, it is beyond the scope of my department.'

The judge paused and looked over at me. 'Mr Cambroe, you have a knack of turning out to be in the right, when at first blush the opposite seems the case. It is, if I may say so, a useful talent. I am overturning the original conviction and dismissing the case with prejudice.'

I felt it was no accident when I encountered Love on the way out. 'You'd better keep your nose clean, Cambroe,' he said.

Peters took the rest of the day off. He and Angel passed the evening in the Phoenix. Due to anxiety surrounding the case the barrister had forgotten to take money with him. He told me to deduct whatever he spent out of his fee.

I got one new customer. His name was Barry the Book. Jack said Barry never worked a day in his entire life. He was a small wiry man of an indeterminate age. He wore a tartan flat cap and a serious expression, both of which he may have had at birth because I never saw him without either. When I enquired how he passed the time, he said, 'Trying to understand the world.'

Barry didn't say much, and would sit at the bar for hours, cap on his head, looking into a pint of beer. I asked him why he was always so quiet. He said he never learned anything when he was talking. When Jack asked him why he liked being in the Phoenix, he answered that everything had phases. 'The moon has phases, life has phases, and my present phase has me going to the Phoenix.'

'Is my bar not being busy also a phase?' I asked.

He looked at me and said, 'Do the seasons change?'

That answer gave me a lift for a little while but nothing could erase Maura from my mind. Jack said there was no way old Creighton would change his mind and therefore no way Maura would marry me. I was better off putting her out of my head, or looking elsewhere if I wanted a partner. Neither of these suggestions were either possible or desired.

One afternoon Jack and I went for a walk by the lake since there was nothing else to do. It was a beautiful day, and children could be heard playing football in the distance. I wasn't noticing any of this. I was just wondering what could be done to increase business. 'The pub should have been named the Misfits Bar,' I said.

'If you could get enough misfits it would be fine,' said Jack.

I was wondering if a misfit would feel at home where everyone else was a misfit, when a child's screeching could be heard coming from up ahead.

We both ran and turned the corner. A bunch of children were shouting and crying and looking into the lake. I grabbed one by the elbow and asked him what had happened.

'Alice Duggan got drowned,' he sobbed.

Several kids shouted, 'Alice Duggan slipped and fell in.'

Even while they were answering me I was ripping off my jacket and jumper and telling Jack to ring 999.

Kicking off my shoes, I dove into the lake. It was still the same as when I was a child. This area was particularly deep with lots of sludge at the bottom. The water was freezing cold, but I didn't notice. The inky blackness was worse. In seconds I was feeling my way in the soft ooze at the bottom of the lake. No sign of anything. I fumbled about in the darkness but then had to come up for air. I surfaced and gasped a couple of lungfuls before going down again. I clawed my way in the dark. Something sticking out of the mud gave me hope for a second, but I realised it was a piece of wood. Then just when I knew I had to surface again, I felt something. I had to get more air. I went up, gulped a deep breath and went straight down again. It was definitely the little girl. Clutching her by the arm, I came up and threw her out onto the embankment. I tossed her over on her back and began giving her the kiss of life. It didn't seem to be having an effect. I turned her on her side and thumped her between the shoulder blades. The little girl's body spasmed and she began to choke. I thumped her again. Now she was vomiting and gasping for air. Some adults had gathered around. The child spluttered and retched, but after a minute her breathing was better.

The child's mother arrived in a frantic state. An ambulance came blaring onto the scene. Jack handed me my clothes.

'Let's get out of here,' I said, 'before I get pneumonia.'

With everyone's attention engrossed on the little girl, no one noticed us slipping away.

The following night I was in the pub with Jack and Podge when ten or twelve people walked in. I didn't know any of them. A man came up to the bar and introduced himself.

'My name is Mick Duggan, the father of Alice whose life you saved yesterday.'

'How is she?'

'Not a bother on her. But that's thanks to you. If it wasn't for what you did we would be having a wake now instead of a celebration.'

'Anyone would do the same,' I said.

'I've heard the gossip about your pub,' said the man, 'and while I'm not big into drinking myself, you have some new customers. This party is on me.'

Later Jack said that the Duggans had wide connections. Barry the Book mumbled something about change being the only constant.

10

One day Jack rang me and said he was taking someone to meet me at my home that night. The stranger was a diminutive man of about seventy who wore his spectacles on his forehead most of the time. I didn't have to be told that he'd been a school teacher. He was introduced as Donald Dunwoody and spoke in a tone that suggested he was teaching me rather than telling me.

Jack said, 'Master Duck has been the principal of Cambroestown school one might say forever, and he is also our local historian.'

'Duck?' I said.

'It's what the pupils used to called me,' said Dunwoody. 'But that's in the past now. Not quite forever, but a long time, alas.'

'He has something to tell you,' said Jack.

We sat down in the drawing room. Dunwoody was looking at everything with great interest.

'You know,' he said, 'it's been maybe forty years since I was in this room, and it still has the same smell.'

'Good or bad?' I asked.

'Neither. Different, I suppose. A kind of old-world smell.'

'Forget about the smell,' said Jack. 'Tell him what you told me.'

The old principal looked at me. I felt like a schoolboy. 'I always taught my students to begin at the beginning. So let's start there.'

'Jesus,' said Jack, groaning in his chair. 'You're not writing a PhD thesis.'

Dunwoody ignored him and continued. 'I was only a college student when this house, this bastion of British imperialism, was liberated by some gallant Irishmen,' he said, a mocking drone to his voice. His sarcasm was refreshing to hear.

'Following the fire and your family's departure it lay derelict for a couple of years. I took up a junior position in the local school and was given permission to investigate the contents of the house for items of historical interest. In one room, I came across bundles of letters in an old trunk. It took me ages to get them sorted, filed and read. Some of them were extremely old.'

'Get to the point, Duck,' said Jack.

Dunwoody fixed his spectacles onto his nose. 'The records show that the land known as the "house fields", now in the possession of Maura Creighton's father, were given by the then occupants of this house, in other words your ancestors, to Maura's great-great-great-grandmother as a gift.'

I sat up at the mention of Maura's name.

Jack must have felt that Dunwoody was going too slow, for he took over. 'The letters will prove that Maura's great-great-great-granny, a girl called Sarah Dawson, worked as a scullery maid in this very building. She was going out with a fellow by the name of Willie Creighton, but it was a doomed affair. Willie had to emigrate to America to seek work. The plan was for Sarah to follow him when he got settled, but things weren't much better in the States. He sent her a letter saying that he hadn't much more status than a slave, that she should stay here and try to get another husband. Now show him the next letter,' he said to Dunwoody.

'This is copied down from the original,' said the old teacher, taking out a piece of paper. 'It has some words missing and others are hard to decipher but here it is.' He passed it to me, and I held it to the light.

'My dear dear Sarah, I have received your last dispatch with heavenly joy. That Captain Cambroe would give you a plot of your own is in the realms of God's goodness. When you wrote that Mistress caught you weeping for me, and that she beseeched her most gracious husband to take the misery from your heart, I could hardly believe that it was true. I will say no more except I pray for you every night, and will now include in my entreatments to the merciful saviour the saintly captain and his mistress. I hope to have saved enough to book my passage home by next year, and we can be married then. Yours ever, Willie.'

When Dunwoody saw that I was finished, he said, 'We think that Sarah must have been a favourite of the mistress of the house.'

'I thought the servants and their masters had no social interaction.'

'Not as a general rule,' he said, 'but often the lady of the big house led an isolated life. Her husband might be in Dublin or overseas, and in some instances she would become friendly with a staff member out of sheer loneliness. Perhaps Sarah had some engaging quality that endeared her to her mistress. In any event, the lady of the manor persuaded her husband to let Sarah have the strip of land running from the back lane down to the edge of the lake where it ends in a narrow point. It wouldn't be missed from an estate of that size, but it was a fortune to a peasant. Twenty acres would grow potatoes and vegetables, allow you to keep goats and cattle. Relevant to the times, Willie and Sarah were rich.'

'The bottom line,' said Jack, 'is that Maura, or Maura's father, or any of the Creightons going right back to poor Willie, would never have existed if it hadn't been for the generosity of Captain Cambroe.'

'Do you think Creighton knows about this?' I asked Dunwoody.

'I don't know. The locals always called those fields "the wee house field" and "the long house field", so it was obvious that they used to belong to the estate. But so did all the other land around here. While the names on the fields stuck, over time the Creightons may have lost knowledge of their family tree. Due to the travails of Irish history, maybe it was deliberately forgotten. Who knows?'

The three of us sat silently for a minute. Then Jack said, 'If Maura's father were to know the history of the land, surely he couldn't refuse you her hand because you are a Cambroe.'

I couldn't think. My head was in turmoil.

Maura had mixed emotions when I told her about it. She

wasn't sure what her father's reaction would be, and she had already almost committed herself to Love.

She arranged for me to meet her father. When he opened the door of his house I was immediately struck by the likeness between him and his daughter. He gave me a firm handshake and welcomed me in. Maura was not present. As instructed by Jack, I acted in a formal manner. He said a traditional approach couldn't do any harm.

'I am here, Mr Creighton, to ask for your daughter's hand in marriage.'

He looked at me for a long moment, then said, 'Maura has told me about the origins of our family history. Let me show you something.'

He took me over to the back window of the bungalow and pointed out to the lake beyond the field. 'When we were children, there was a family legend that half of that lake belonged to the Creightons by right. I know now how that story arose.'

'There must be deeds going back that would show how you came to own this land,' I said.

Creighton shook his head. 'I have been mulling this over. There are no deeds for this property. There was never a need. It was handed on from father to eldest son. When the big house people gave the land to Sarah Dawson they owned everything. All that was required was for them to say you can have that strip of ground. Maybe Sarah was only lent the land. How would you know? But over time it was accepted that my family were the legal owners. Maybe we were also given half of the lake to fish in, which is where the legend might have come from, but you can't occupy water the same as a firm piece of ground.'

He told me to sit and asked if I wanted tea or coffee. I said tea to be on the safe side.

'You know all these revelations have solved a dilemma for me,' old Creighton said as he came in carrying a tray of china cups and saucers with matching jug and sugar bowl. 'But first have some tea. Maybe I should have offered you a drink?'

'No, tea is fine,' I said.

I thought I detected a nod of approval at this.

As he poured the tea, Creighton said, 'It's not often I get to use these. They were a wedding present for me and Sarah, may the Lord have mercy on her dear soul.'

I was wondering at the coincidence of his wife being called Sarah as well, when he leaned back in his chair and said, 'I need to explain something to you. There are things you don't know about.'

'Tell me,' I said. 'I want to know.'

'Attitudes towards the people in the big house in all parts of Ireland changed with the times, and with the way their occupants treated the peasants. Cambroestown was no different. I don't have any specific knowledge that your family were bad landlords, but I was reared in the politics of an age that took a dim view of English gentry in Ireland. For Christ's sake, your father and mother were burned out of the house. Maybe I was brainwashed, but I always took the view that that was a right and proper thing to do.'

It was galling to hear him say it, but I knew that he was just being honest.

He took a drink of tea. 'How could I in all conscience let

those same gentry come back and take over my wee holding, which you marrying Maura would have meant?'

I was about to interrupt when he put up his hand. 'Let me finish. I love my daughter more than anything in the world. Every time I look at her I see her mother. I would do anything possible to make her happy, and it's clear she loves you. But to give her my permission to marry a Cambroe, someone who nobody knows anything about, was too much to ask. Plus I know Sergeant Love would make her a good steady husband.'

I had trouble biting my tongue. There was silence for a few seconds. I could see the old man was gearing himself up to say something more.

'What has come to light changes everything. Can I stop the wheel of life?'

'What do you mean?' I said.

'Your marrying my daughter would mean Cambroe to Cambroe in so many generations. You may not think much of my few little fields, Mr Cambroe, but in Ireland land is everything.'

'Mr Creighton, of course I know the importance of your land.'

'That would be a comfort to me,' he said.

'I respect its significance.'

Creighton got out of the chair and walked to the window overlooking the lake. Gazing through the glass, he said, 'I'm still ignorant of your personal background, Mr Cambroe.' Then he turned and held my eye. 'But in the light of what we now know, and because I want my beloved Maura to get her wish, I am prepared to give you permission to marry my daughter.'

Six weeks later Maura and I got married. We had about twenty people at the wedding, which we held in a small hotel in Dublin so as not to create a furore on Sergeant Love's patch. He wasn't too happy about it but that was only to be expected. Most of the guests were her pals. Since Mickey Patton was my oldest friend he was best man. A workmate of Maura's was bridesmaid. My other guests were Jack, Podge and Barry the Book At the wedding breakfast, Mickey gave a speech.

He said, 'It can be argued that it's unfair that someone would come from Australia to claim Cambroestown's biggest prize, but it isn't so. My boyhood friend's body may have been in that faraway land, but his soul never left Monaghan.'

Someone shouted, 'Up Monaghan!'

'He's as welcome home as the primroses that grow along our ditches in May. And as for the bride, has there ever been one so lovely to behold? Why, I would have married her myself . . . if I'd thought of it.'

Everyone knew that Mickey had been infatuated with Maura, and there was a generous laugh. Mickey called a toast for the bride and groom, and then Podge stood up.

'I just want to say a couple of sentences,' he began. 'I want to wish Josie and Maura all happiness in their marriage, and to express the hope that the joy of their union bear a similarity to the wished for union between the two parts of our beloved nation.'

'Then how would you make a living?' shouted Jack,

amidst much laughter.

I almost felt drunk with happiness. Not alone had I won Maura, I had good friends. The banter among them was a pleasure to watch. At one stage Micky's dexterity with one hand was the centre of attention. He could do something that in all my travels I never saw before, and that was flip the lid off a bottle of beer with the thumb of his hand. I had seen guys do it with their teeth, usually drunk, but never like Mickey could do it. Everyone was amazed at how he had built up the strength in his remaining hand to compensate for the loss of the other. Podge suggested luring some innocent to bet that it couldn't be done. Jack wondered if it would be legal to win a bet like that. Barry the Book said greed was man's fundamental weakness, and that the law never stopped people trying to make a handy pound. Mickey, to his credit, shot the idea down and called for another round on him. Podge was disappointed, saying one must use all of one's talents to their best advantage. The day passed in a flash. It had to have been the best day of my life.

Maura and I spent our wedding night in the Gresham. She had been so excited by it on our last visit, I wanted her to have the experience of staying there. She was most impressed by the en-suite bathroom that had both a shower and a bath, and also the size of the bed.

She insisted on lying across it instead of up and down just for fun. When I put my arms around her she was very shy, and said she didn't have any previous experience of this sort of thing. Later, when I said, 'For one who had no experience, you were a quick learner,' she punched me in the belly before hugging me to her tightly.

Then she abruptly jumped out of the bed and got on her knees. I watched her in amazement.

Out loud she began to pray. 'For this day I want to thank our Lord Jesus. I want to thank Sarah Dawson. I want to thank Willie Creighton. I want to thank Captain and Mrs Cambroe. I want to thank my father and mother.' Then she blessed herself and jumped back into the bed and put her arms around me.

'I am going to say those prayers every night of my life for as long as I live,' she said, and began kneading the back of my neck with her hands.

'That's nice,' I said. 'You should become a masseur.'

Maura laughed. 'I don't think there'd be much of a market in Monaghan for a masseur. Imagine an oul' farmer coming in and taking off his clothes so that a woman could rub him all over with oil. I'd be read from the altar.'

'At least you'd be famous.'

'Infamous like yourself more like.' She pressed her body tightly against me. 'Please hold me,' she said.

We toured Ireland for five days and stopped in B&Bs. None of them had en-suite rooms. The strangest aspect of them was the attitude of the lady of the house. We quickly learned it was necessary for Maura to flash her wedding ring if we didn't want to be met with suspicion and furtive looks. I asked Maura why they were so worried whether we were married or not as it was us that was committing the sin and not them. She said if we were not married they would be just as guilty for allowing us to sleep together under their roof.

On one of the days we visited the Cliffs of Moher. They

were magnificent – blue skies, blustering wind, and seagulls wheeling in wide circles. There were very few people about. 'Away out there is America,' I said.

We walked along the edge of the precipice and gazed down at the waves far below crashing into the sides of the rock face. I held Maura's hand and felt her shiver. 'If you fell off the edge, no one would ever know,' she said.

In Mayo, Maura showed me a holy mountain that people climbed every year. I told her of the Aborigines in Australia and their holy places. Also in Mayo, she brought me to Knock, which was where she had teased Mickey about visiting on his weekends away. When I looked at the less than fertile landscape of much of Mayo, I could understand the people's plight a hundred years before. It gave me a deeper appreciation of the value of a small field in such times.

After we got home I felt that I had to call to Dunwoody and thank him. Without his discovery, I never could have married Maura.

He greeted me warmly. 'Come into my den,' he said.

His den turned out to be a huge room with stacks of old newspapers placed all around the walls, in some cases almost reaching the ceiling. The year that each pile related to was stuck on the front. Facing these were boxes and boxes of papers, again with a year clearly marked on the side. In the middle of the room sat a desk and a couple of easy chairs. Beside the desk were a row of tall filing cabinets. The drawers were closed, but I knew the enclosed files would have been just as organised as everything else.

I stood there and took in the scene, not knowing if I was more impressed by the amount of material the Duck had, or his classification system. He was a man of order and structure. Then it hit me. Why hadn't I thought of it before? This man had the whole history of the area right here in this room. He would surely have some information on the burning of Cambroestown House.

'Please sit down,' said Dunwoody. 'Strangers are always surprised at what I call my bookkeeping system. If it were any other way, chaos would reign supreme. What are you having? Brandy, whiskey, port perhaps?'

'A cup of coffee will be fine,' I said.

Dunwoody went to the door and shouted into the kitchen. 'Kathleen, darling, would you ever bring in a pot of coffee for two?'

He said to me, 'My long suffering wife. She never comes in here except when I want something.'

Kathleen carried in a tray of cups and saucers. 'The truth is he won't allow me here in case I disturb his precious archives,' she said setting out the crockery.

'You know, my sweet, that you're the most precious thing in my life.'

Kathleen mumbled something as she left.

'I am very impressed,' I said looking around the room. 'You should have been a professional historian.'

'Job vacancies for historians are few and far between. Anyway, I hate the subject as much as I love it.'

'Why is that?'

'History by definition is always in the past, and there is never an absolute truth that one can reach. People construct narratives to suit what they want to believe. Stop a loyal Orangeman marching down the Shankill Road on the twelfth of July and tell him that at the Battle of the Boyne King Billy was fighting on the side of the pope. And if you survive that, inform him that he is marching on the wrong day, that the battle wasn't fought on the twelfth but on the first of July. History is presented as a struggle between goodies and baddies. But there are rarely any goodies; just baddies who are designated goodies. Were the people who burnt out your family goodies or baddies? What would old Creighton have said before he knew the truth?'

Just then Kathleen came in with a pot of coffee and began pouring it out. 'Don't let him confuse you,' she said to me. 'His mind is as likely to be in the seventeenth century as the twentieth.'

'Speaking of old Creighton,' I said, 'that is why I am here. To thank you for your revelations.'

'I'm only too happy for you.' He waved his arm around the room. 'It's rare that any of this stuff is of interest to anyone but myself.'

'Now that I see it,' I said, 'can I ask you a question?'

'Fire away.'

'Would you have any information to do with the night the house was burned?'

Dunwoody had been about to take a drink from the cup. He hesitated for a second before continuing. Then he set the cup down on the saucer and fixed the spoon carefully beside it. 'It would be wrong of me if I said I hadn't expected this question. In fact I was a little bit surprised you never mentioned it the night we met.'

‘I was too taken up with Maura and her father, then the wedding, and then the honeymoon.’

‘I understand only too well. However, I don’t know if I can help you very much.’

He got out of the chair and went to a filing cabinet. He pulled open a drawer and took out a huge folder of old newspapers.

‘Ever since I heard that a Cambroe was back in the big house, I have been conducting some research.’ He spread the newspapers across his desk. ‘There wasn’t much to go on except contemporaneous news reports, and they weren’t going to name any names. There is a small account of the fire at Cambroestown House, but it doesn’t give much information. Only that a number of men carried it out and that this type of activity was now prevalent throughout the land. Can you remember the number of men involved or anything of that nature?’

I said that sometimes I had visions of the event. A long thin guy with a limp urging the others to burn the house to the ground.

Dunwoody looked at me. ‘A limp?’

‘I know the Fling Devlin has a limp, and he was active at the time. But he got that injury at the very end of the war, long after my family was burned out.’

Dunwoody rose from where he was sitting and began walking along the stacks of newspapers. I could tell he was checking the year marked on each. He stopped at one pile, lifted some papers off the top and set them to one side. After looking at the dates some more, he chose one and brought it over to the desk.

'Read this.'

The headline said, 'New TD elected for Monaghan constituency.'

'See what it says about him in his profile,' said Dunwoody.

I found the small paragraph near the bottom. 'The new representative had to cope with serious illness as a child when he suffered from polio. Although left with a severe limp in his right leg, Devlin never let this handicap get in the way of his efforts to free Ireland.'

'The Fling,' I murmured. 'But everyone here believes he was the last man to have been shot during the troubles.'

'You weren't listening to what I said about truth and history,' said Dunwoody. 'The Fling fostered that notion in speeches until it became accepted as truth. This article is probably the only existing account of the real facts. I have always known he didn't get the limp from being shot. If one of the guys who burned your house had a limp, then I'm sure it was him. I have seen loads of speeches where he alludes to his part in the burning of big houses, without ever actually saying so. Not only that, he boasts of being the head of his unit in this area. He would have directed whatever operations they were involved in. There's only one conclusion. Not only was the Fling at the burning of your house, he was the leader of the gang.'

I didn't know what to say. The implications left me dumbfounded.

'I have been researching stuff my whole life,' said Dunwoody, seeing my confusion. 'I know all accepted history is suspect and should be treated with caution. Yet when one comes across a blatant example of past events being modified to suit causes and people, it still has the power to amaze.'

I remained silent, trying to process what I had just learned.

Dunwoody said, 'Josie,' and he waited for me to look at him. 'It's really none of my business, but it would be remiss of me if I didn't remind you that knowledge can sometimes be a dangerous thing, especially if a piece of information is a threat to someone else. Harm can occur in ways never dreamt of.'

Kathleen rapped on the door and asked if we wanted more coffee. I told them it was time I was going. Really I wanted to be alone to get my head cleared and think.

I told Dunwoody that it was thanks to him I had a wife who would be waiting on me. He walked me to my car. Before I got in he shook my hand and said, 'Don't forget Socrates' advice, Josie.'

'What was that?'

Dunwoody gripped my hand firmly. 'Never return an injury.'

11

Locals gradually started to frequent the Phoenix. Just one or two at the start, then some nights there would be maybe five or six people. On one occasion I counted twenty customers, all from around the village. The Fling Devlin arrived in one night with a number of party hacks. He was full of bonhomie and good humour as he ordered a round for his friends. When the drinks had been served, he turned around and began addressing the rest of the customers as if he was on stage making a speech.

'Ireland is the land of welcomes and opportunity. We hail the visitor, the tourist, the businessman, the entrepreneur, and the returned emigrant all equally. My friend here, the owner of this fine establishment, Mr Cambroe, fits into several of these categories, which is all the more reason we want to congratulate him on his success.' Then in a pretend whisper to a sidekick, he said, 'Government policy is working. Look at the numbers in here all spending money,' which raised a laugh among his companions and somewhat less with the rest of the customers. He continued, 'I never knew our genial host before he left for foreign climes, as he was then just a boy. His manner of leaving was unfortunate but times were different then. Our little country has come a long way since those regrettable events. That said, for me personally that period gave me an opportunity to do my bit, as the saying goes. The most famous son of another of our emigrants put it better than me when he invited people to ask what you can do for your country. I felt I wanted to ask that question. Friends, the next round of drinks are on the Fling.'

I watched the Fling's performance in disgust. Some people even clapped. Later, after I had the place cleared, Jack said it was a canvassing stunt. The Fling had inside knowledge to do with the timing of the election.

On account of the way the Phoenix had taken off, I decided I should hold a little party for my four original regulars. I announced that due to the increase in business, Maura would be working full-time in the bar. She had handed in her notice in the hotel – something I was glad of. I hated her being away from me. Maybe she would have an accident on the road. Maybe Soapie would let down her tyres. It was better she stayed home where I could look after her. The truth was I just wanted to be with her all the time The party was a quiet affair. Podge spent the evening moaning he would have to find another quiet hole to hide out in as the customs would be sniffing around soon. Barry stared into a half empty glass most of the time. Jack enjoyed his pint. Angel, a natural organiser, proposed we enter a quiz team in the annual pub quiz tournament. This was agreed. They assured me it was always a ferociously contested event with the winners held in high esteem in the locality.

The members of the quiz team would be Jack, Podge, Barry, and myself. Jack, being a barrister, was highly educated. Podge had great local knowledge. Barry, even though the answers had to be dragged out of him, had read almost everything, and the theory was that I possessed a huge amount of general knowledge because of my travels. Angel was team manager. The league was run on a home and away basis, with the final to be played between the winners and the runners up. Donaghy's had won the competition for the past two years. Their captain was Johnny Crowley, the oldest of the Crowley brothers.

As the competition progressed the Phoenix performed well and won all their matches. So too did Donaghy's. When the Donaghy's team had to visit my pub there was standing room only for the local derby. It was great for business and also made people make up their minds as to who they were supporting. My team were beaten comprehensively on the night, but in the return match the Phoenix won narrowly, thus the final between the two pubs was set up. It would be held in the Práta Tavern – neutral ground.

In the period leading up to it, the chief topic of conversation in both premises was the playoff. There were lots of rumours. It was said Donaghy's had enlisted two quiz specialists from Belfast to play on their team. I didn't believe this because it would look bad if they had to go outside their own customer base. A particularly nasty story had it that Angel was using her charms on the quizmaster to find out what questions were going to be asked. I didn't know if Angel heard any of this gossip, but she had the Phoenix team practising for two hours each evening. She borrowed books on every conceivable subject from the local library. To speed things up, when Barry was asked a question he would either give a thumbs up or a thumbs down instead of a verbal reply. This indicated if he knew the answer or not.

On the night itself the lounge in the Práta was packed. A stage had been erected so everyone had a view. The quizmaster was seated at a table placed in front of the two teams. A precise little man with a Hitler type moustache, he displayed an air of authority by continually shuffling the questions.

Quiz aficionados from all around the area were present. They would mentally try to answer every question, and if wrong, take on board the correct answer for future reference. The chat was similar to what goes on prior to a football match. 'It's anyone's game.' 'You need to get the rub of the green.' 'It's all according to form on the night.' None of Donaghy's team ever touched alcohol prior to a game. Podge insisted on having a couple of pints, to relieve the tension and help him relax. Other than the neutral spectators, I was perhaps the most calm person in the room. Regardless of the outcome, my pub had been established in the community. Donaghy's had more to lose than me.

As the match progressed the score was close. I was surprised that so many of the questions had come up in our practice sessions. It proved Angel's argument that quizzes weren't about intelligence – the more you participated in them, the better you would be. Donaghy's had a long tradition of taking part in quizzes so they had a huge advantage.

In spite of that, the Phoenix held its own, and if Barry answered the last question correctly it would be a draw. In this event the rules were that one team member would be matched against an opposite number in a sudden death playoff. Barry's question was, 'How would you tell the difference between a female pheasant and male pheasant?'

Practically everyone in the room would know that the male had lovely bright plumage and the female dull sandy coloured feathers. The question was simple, but Barry wasn't a simple man. 'I would watch which one laid the eggs,' he said.

I never found out if he said this on purpose or not, because it was a legitimate answer, if not the one the quizmaster had on his sheet. After the pandemonium had settled, the quizmaster decided he had to accept the answer as valid. The teams were all square.

Although I was the weakest member of my team, the others didn't want to take responsibility for losing, and I was put forward. 'In any case,' said Jack, 'at this stage it's pure chance.'

My opponent would be Donaghy's team captain, Johnny Crowley.

All the rest of the team members withdrew. Crowley and I sat facing each other. After a toss of a coin, Donaghy's man was first to go. Crowley, his eyes closed and fists clenched, exuded total focus. I tried to clear my mind. The quizmaster coughed politely and asked Crowley, 'How many items are in a baker's dozen?'

I thanked God that I hadn't been asked that question. I never heard of a baker's dozen.

'Thirteen,' he answered.

A big hurrah was heard from among the audience. It was Soapie Crowley. Now it was my turn. 'How many thousands are there in a million?' asked the quizmaster.

'One thousand,' I answered.

There were cheers from my supporters.

The quizmaster turned and faced Crowley. 'What is the largest stretch of fresh water in the British Isles?'

Crowley smiled. He realised the question could have been asked in a more simple manner: 'What is the largest lake in the British Isles?'

'Lough Neagh,' he said. 'But there's nothing British about it.'

Again there were raucous cheers coming from the audience.

'Ok, Josie,' said the quizmaster. 'Where would you find the Sea of Tranquillity?'

Now it was my turn to smile. This question had come up in one of Angel's practice sessions. 'On the moon,' I said, to clapping from Phoenix followers.

'At this rate I'm going to run out of questions.' The quizmaster turned back to Crowley. 'What would a fisherman do with a priest?'

Crowley grimaced and screwed up his face. Many of the questions were chosen so as to allow smart interjections from the audience. But this being the final, the 'wits' kept their answers to themselves. I let my eyes wander around the audience to project an air of confidence. I noticed Angel with an empty glass in her hand, which was something I'd never seen before.

I knew the answer to the question, which was a bad omen. Now I probably wouldn't know my own question. Crowley seemed stuck. Someone could be heard striking a match to light their cigarette.

'Ten seconds,' said the quizmaster. A few moments later, he said, 'Time's up. The answer is that he would use it to kill a fish he had just caught. A priest is the name given to a club used for that purpose.'

There was a sudden explosion of noise. Soapie Crowley was livid. 'You're a fucking dummy,' he shouted at his brother.

'Quiet everyone,' hollered the quizmaster.

A hush settled down again. Now it was my turn. This would be my best, maybe my only chance. No way would Crowley miss two questions in a row if it went to a fourth round. The quizmaster cleared his throat. 'What bird,' he said, very slowly and precisely, 'hatches its eggs standing on its feet?'

My heart sank. I had no idea. A 'bird' being a name commonly given to girls, it was a question that facilitated all kinds of rude responses. But there was also a correct answer and I didn't know it. I remembered a discussion one evening when Jack said, 'There's no point in thinking about it. You either know an answer or you don't.' Angel had argued that was wrong. There were some questions that if you thought about them for a second you would get an answer. I closed my eyes and concentrated as hard as I could. A bird that hatches its eggs standing on its feet must have very short legs.

'Ten seconds,' said the quizmaster.

I had no idea where the answer came from. 'A penguin,' I shouted.

'Correct answer,' said the quizmaster, and bedlam broke

out. My supporters were on their feet cheering and clapping. I reached out to shake Crowley's hand. Crowley took it even though Soapie was shouting to his brother, 'Don't shake the bastard's hand, Johnny.'

During the presentation of the prizes, Soapie poured out a torrent of abuse not only on myself but also on the other members of the team. He called Jack an oddball as he was receiving the trophy. He shouted out that Podge was a Northern gangster, and that Barry was a stuttering idiot. Angel was told to go home to her husband. Eventually his brothers managed to get him out of the pub. By that time our supporters and myself were heading back to the Phoenix anyway.

On the way I reminded myself to be careful. Moments like these were dangerous for me, when it would be so easy to slip up. Times of joy and times of sorrow were to be handled with caution.

When we reached home I placed the trophy – a copper statue of Cú Chulainn, the legendary Irish warrior – on a prominent shelf behind the bar. Maura was over the moon. She had stayed back to mind the place, saying the tension at the quiz would be too much for her.

'Remember the first few times we met I was always asking you quiz questions?' she said. 'You've come a long way IQ-wise since arriving in Monaghan.'

Barry, ignoring the singing and yahooing, sat at the bar looking into his pint. Every so often I stopped what I was doing to admire the trophy. 'It's great, isn't it,' I said to Barry.

'It is now,' said Barry.

'What do you mean it is now?'

'Everything changes.'

'Oh yeah? What's going to change?'

'Everything,' said Barry.

A shiver ran through me as though someone had walked on my grave. I put my arm around Maura's waist to reassure myself.

12

A few days later Angel came into the bar. I was on my own stocking up the shelves.

'That's it at last,' she said.

I looked up and saw she was flushed but sober. 'What do you mean?'

'I had a huge row with my husband. I am leaving him. It had to happen sooner or later.'

'I'm sorry,' I said.

Angel slumped into a chair saying, 'Well, I'm not. Our marriage has been over for a long time.'

'Where are you going to go?'

'I don't know. That's actually my main concern.'

'Wait,' I said, lifting the phone. I rang Maura, told her about Angel and then mentioned all the space we had in our house. There were a couple of rooms a little bit apart from the rest. If they were aired and dusted down they would solve Angel's problem. Maura agreed saying they were not being used for anything else. Angel was delighted with the arrangement.

Maura suggested to me that I should go and see Angel's husband. Maybe her involvement with the quiz team led to the breakup. If that was the case, I needed to clear the air.

He met me at the door, very cordial, but he didn't invite me in saying the house was in a mess. Small in stature, he struck me as an inoffensive type who would accept whatever the world threw at him. I told him Angel had mentioned to me that she was leaving. I wanted to assure him that if her participation in bar activates was in any way to blame, I would tell her to stay away from the Phoenix. He shook his head and said she would only find another pub. 'It's maybe better this way. Whatever will be will be.'

He was silent for a couple of seconds as if wondering should he say more, then he said, 'Angel always wanted children, and we never had any. I think she has been trying to bury that disappointment in drinking and running around. I can't give her what she wants. Alcoholics, when they drink, are totally different people to when they are sober, and at this stage I no longer have any feelings for her.' He looked at me and said earnestly, 'Alcohol kills everything.'

I nodded and said, 'I'm sorry.'

Maura and I were making love. When we did so it was as if she was supplying a part of me that had always been missing. It gave me a sense of wholeness, and like having some kind of spiritual experience I didn't want the feeling to end.

The front door bell rang. Someone was holding their finger on it. The strident demand for attention shattered the idyllic. 'Let it ring,' said Maura.

I was going to agree with her but knew there was no point. It was just going to keep on ringing. When I opened the door, I saw that Love and Dooley were the culprits.

'What is it now, Sergeant Love?' I said as evenly as I could muster.

'Can we come in, Mr Cambroe,' said the policeman.

I took them in but didn't offer them anything. They didn't sit down, and I waited to hear what they wanted.

'I will get to the point,' said Love. 'You had a wedding reception in the Swan Hotel in Dublin recently.'

I shifted uncomfortably and wondered how he was coping with losing Maura.

'Everyone knows that,' I said.

'A waitress in that hotel has been murdered. It is suspected that the murderer is the same person who murdered the prostitute.'

'Why?'

'Because she had been hacked up in a similar fashion.'

Dooley set himself on the edge of a chair. 'It would appear there is a connection between these murders and you. Perhaps someone is trying to get you into trouble?'

'Who would go to that extreme to get me into trouble?'

Just then Maura entered the room in her dressing gown. She started when she saw who it was and tightened the belt on her gown unconsciously.

Love stared at her for a second before regaining his composure. 'Good morning, Maura,' he said politely. 'I am sorry if I have got you out of bed.'

I almost felt sorry for Love. It couldn't have been easy for him losing a prize like Maura.

'Good morning, John, and good morning, Detective. It's time to be up anyway,' she said. 'I will put on the kettle. Would either of you like some breakfast?'

'No, we will be on our way soon.'

'A waitress at our wedding reception hotel has been murdered,' I told Maura.

She let out a little gasp. 'That's terrible,' she said. 'I wonder which one it was?'

'Her name was Bridget,' said Love. 'She had long dark hair tied in a bun I believe.'

'I don't remember her,' said Maura. 'But it's been three months since our wedding. Was she working there then?'

'She's been there twelve years.'

'It's so sad,' said Maura.

'I remember asking you before if you had any enemies,' Love said to me.

'You know as well as I do about Soapie Crowley. I guess you could class him as an enemy. Have you questioned him? Nobody has been charged with the burning of my bar.'

'Do you think Soapie started the fire?' said Dooley reaching into his inside pocket for a little compact case. He opened it and took out his trademark nail-file. I knew a priest one time who always had a handkerchief in his hand and would wind it around his hand when under pressure, which was often in the community he served. He would leave it sitting on the altar when saying mass.

'Someone started it, and it wasn't me in case you have ideas in that direction,' I said to Love.

'I have never suggested it was you,' said the sergeant.

I didn't reply.

'Are you sure you won't have tea?' said Maura.

'No thanks,' said Love. 'We'll be on our way. Anyway a murder away up in Dublin shouldn't really be any concern of ours. But we get directions to check these things out because of the hand in the field.'

He was being more polite than usual, and it must have been on account of Maura's presence.

After the pair had left, Maura said, 'I don't think Soapie would do such unspeakable things. Murdering someone like that is the act of a madman.'

'I agree with you,' I said, taking her in my arms. 'Now where were we when we got interrupted.'

I had been invited to a meeting by the local brass-band. Their intention was to have a weekend festival in the village to raise funds for the band and to celebrate their music. A number of bands from surrounding areas would take part and it would be a fun weekend for everyone. I was delighted to be asked to attend as it would integrate me more into the community. It was decided this would be a non-political event, so Fling, who would only be too keen to head the committee, was not invited. I had not stopped thinking about Fling and what he had done to my family. I spent hours musing on how I would confirm it was him, or how I might confront him or deal with it.

Donaghy was at the meeting and we exchanged pleasantries. The Crowley brothers were also there, but not Soapie. There were reports of him going on heavy drinking binges. The brothers gave me a curt hello, which I responded to in a similar fashion. I spoke very little during the meeting and went along with the various suggestions that were made. I would help with erecting the bunting, and on the Saturday night hold a huge soirée in my bar that would involve various bands performing in the big lounge.

On Sunday night the winners would be presented with their medals in Donaghy's place.

On my way home from the meeting, the engine of my jeep started to splutter and eventually stopped. I was forced to abandon it and walk home. When I towed it into the local garage the next morning, we discovered as much as two pounds of sugar had been poured into the fuel tank. The garage man said I had been very lucky the engine wasn't banjaxed.

Love kept me waiting. When I was finally admitted to his office he didn't say hello, and before I had a chance to speak, he said, 'Mr Cambroe, if you had a twin we would have to employ more staff in this station.'

'Sergeant, you're going to have to do something about Soapie.'

'What's happened now?'

I told him about the fuel in my jeep being contaminated.

'How do you know it was Soapie that did it?'

'Who else would it be?'

Love shrugged his shoulders. 'Who can say?'

'Can you not arrest him and take him in for questioning?'

'Let me explain something to you, Mr Cambroe. The Crowleys are highly respected in this community. Now Soapie may be a bit of a renegade, but the rest of the family would be much aggrieved that one of them was arrested and taken to the barracks. I couldn't do so without firm evidence. Suspicion alone does not suffice.'

'Is there not such a thing as circumstantial evidence?'

'What circumstantial evidence? That he doesn't like you

because you bought the big house and land? No, Mr Cambroe. You will have to provide me with more than that. Now, I am a very busy man. Good day to you.'

As I was opening the door to leave I turned back to him. 'Is it me or you that's the policeman? Surely it is your job to find the evidence, not mine.'

I closed the door behind me before he had a chance to reply.

For the next six weeks I was heavily involved in helping to organise the festival. An in-house committee comprised of Jack, Podge and Angel helped get the Phoenix ready for the pipe band competition on the Saturday night. The plan was that all the bands would compete and play in the village square during the day with the three finalists competing again in my place for first, second and third. Our main problem in the bar was getting enough space, but we were confident of it being a success.

On Sunday, all the bands would perform in the open air and the medal ceremony would be held in Donaghy's that night. The village had been decorated with bunting, and when Saturday arrived there was a great atmosphere. It turned out to be a beautiful summer day, enhancing the carnival atmosphere. Chip vans, hamburger vans, baked potato stalls and hotdog stands emitted delicious aromas. The pipe bands blasted tunes both stirring and sad. A funfair with a big wheel was the centre of attraction for parents with children. I was helping out as a steward while staff were manning the bar. Towards evening, I went in to my place for a cup of coffee. Maura called me into the kitchen and closed the door.

'Sit down,' she said.

'I can't chat. I have to get back out there,' I said, standing at the table and gulping down the coffee.

'I'm pregnant,' said Maura.

'What?'

'I'm pregnant.'

'You're what?'

'Pregnant.'

'Oh my God.'

I wasn't sure I was hearing right. Maura was laughing, enjoying my reaction.

'When did you find out? Why did you not tell me before now? When is it due? Are you really, really sure?'

'Woah there, one question at a time.'

I jumped up and hugged her. 'Oh, I love you so much. This is the best day of my life.'

'I was looking forward to telling you,' said Maura, 'but I wanted it to be when things were going great, which they are today.'

'Can I run out and tell everyone?'

'This is our affair. You can tell our friends later.'

The next few hours were a blur to me. In spite of what Maura said, I couldn't keep quiet about it and told Jack, Podge and Angel right away. Angel said there will be drinks on the house tonight. Then we had to get organised for the bands playing indoors. By evening time the place was packed and everything was running along nicely in an organised chaotic kind of way. The first band played and the judges made their notes. Then the second band marched to the centre of the floor and performed their programme. At that stage we had to close the doors and only open them to let people out. People were jammed together inside like sardines. I was just organising the departure of the second band when there was an urgent banging on the front door. When I opened it there were several gardaí standing outside and three garda cars parked on the road with blue lights flashing.

Love was there. 'You have to clear the premises immediately,' he said. 'We have received a phone call that a bomb has been left in the building.'

'What? It's a hoax,' I said, 'and it's going to disrupt everything.'

'We can't take the chance. Are you going to clear the premises now or do I have to arrest you for obstruction?'

There was no point in arguing even though I suspected it was Soapie up to his tricks again. I went inside, got a microphone and asked everyone to leave as quietly as possible, that there had been a bomb warning. Most people were reluctant to go but the gardaí hurried them along. In minutes the place was empty. Then the gardaí went in and began searching for a suspect device. I wondered if they would be so brave if they really believed there was a bomb hidden somewhere. Love advised people not to hang around as it was going to take quite a while before the all-clear could be given. A hastily organised committee meeting decided that the band finals would be held outdoors the next day.

Even during the scare, Maura's pregnancy was foremost in my mind. Our busiest day ever being spoiled could not ruin my joy. After a couple of hours searching every nook and cranny of the pub, the gardaí declared the place safe. By now, the only people still about were Jack and Podge. Angel had disappeared somewhere, almost certainly to another pub, but returned later on for the celebrations.

We did celebrate for some hours, and talked about the bomb scare, although I could hardly wait to take Maura home and be alone with her.

When I went to open the bar the next day, I saw Dooley walking along the street. After exchanging the time of day with him, I said, 'Did you really need to close the pub because of some anonymous telephone call?'

'We can't take chances.'

'Who would want to put a bomb in my place? And anyway, the only people who have bombs are the IRA, and I understood they had ceased their campaign.'

'There's a well-known IRA sympathiser who hangs out in the Phoenix,' said Dooley.

I knew he was talking about Podge. 'He's hardly likely to be blowing up the place.'

'The bomb could have been intended for somewhere else and had to be dumped for some reason.'

'Do you honestly believe that?'

'No,' said Dooley, 'but we have to take into account all possibilities when we get a warning such as this.'

'Who do you think was really responsible?' I said.

'We pursue all lines of enquiry.'

'You know I'm being harassed by Soapie Crowley. He has to be the main suspect.'

He didn't answer me, except to say he was sorry for my

loss of business on the night. He got into his car and drove away. As I watched him go, I decided to have a talk with Jack about Soapie.

'Ah, Mother's milk,' said Jack after taking the first mouthful from a pint of Guinness. He set it down on the table in front of him. 'Ok, let's discuss what might be called the Soapie question.'

'We have to get him to stop his capers some way. Could we go above Sergeant Love and take my concerns to an inspector or someone of higher rank?'

Jack smiled at me. 'You think Love hassles you now? If you went above his head, it would be like squaring up to a grizzly bear instead of a sheep. He would crucify you.'

'I have to do something,'

'What about giving Soapie a bit of a hiding?'

'I'm a quiet type.'

'You're what? What would the Crowleys have thought after the barn dance?'

'Maybe, but I have had my fill of hitting people.'

'What about Podge? He's bound to know a few hard geezers who wouldn't be too difficult to shoe?'

'What do you mean, "shoe"?'

'Pay, reward, recompense.'

I shook my head. 'I will catch my own kangaroo.'

Jack laughed. 'That won't be easy in Monaghan.'

He took another swallow from his pint. 'I have it,' he said. 'I read somewhere recently that James Cagney was the quietest, most inoffensive man you could meet.'

'Are you drunk or something? What has James Cagney

got to do with the Soapie problem?'

'Cagney could *pretend* to be the bad guy better than anyone. Do you remember this?' Jack pointed both index fingers in the shape of two guns, and said, '*You dirty rat.*'

The imitation was so was so bad I had to smile.

'When it comes to brains,' said Jack, 'Einstein has nothing to fear from Soapie. You could just do a bit of acting. You wouldn't have to lay a finger on him.'

I thought about it for a moment. Maybe it could work.

'Do your Cagney again,' I said.

I knew Soapie's brothers took his car keys from him most nights and made him walk home from Donaghy's in case he had an accident. I had a loan of Jack's car, and when I saw Soapie leave the bar I drove past him and stopped. He would imagine it was someone giving him a lift. Clearly well drunk, he had opened the car door and was sitting in before he focused on me. He gave a gasp. I took off.

'I wanted to talk to you,' I said, putting a slur on my speech and pressing down hard on the accelerator. At Soapie's feet there were a couple of empty whiskey bottles.

'What about?' he stammered.

'Don't fret,' I said. 'I'm not going to hurt you.' I let the steering wheel slip through my fingers a little. The car veered towards a lamppost, and I only righted it when Soapie flinched and covered his face.

'Jesus,' he muttered.

'You know all those stories you heard of the things I done in Australia?' I said. 'Murdering people and cutting them to pieces and everything?'

I turned my head to look at him, even though I knew there was a sharp bend coming.

'Keep your eye on the fuckin' road!' he cried.

I let the car swerve around the corner. 'Well, have you heard them?'

'Yes,' he said, his hands gripping the seat.

'Just between you and me, I'm actually ok when I'm sober.'

I saw Soapie glance down at the empty liquor bottles. Jack was right about this guy. He really wasn't the brightest star in the Milky Way.

'I want you,' I said, 'to confess all the things you've done on me, and promise never to hassle me again.'

Soapie's face had blotches of red and white, flushed from alcohol and drained with fear.

'I promise,' he said, 'on my mother's grave I won't do anything more.'

'Tell me all the things you've done.'

As we roared through the countryside, the tyres squealing on each turn, Soapie sang like a nightingale. He couldn't speak fast enough. 'I started the fire in your pub. I put sugar in your petrol tank. I stole timber and cement from your renovation site,' he blabbered out, which was something I didn't know about. 'I called in the hoax bomb scare.' He went on and on and then said that was everything.

I asked him about the dead dog left on my porch.

'I don't know anything about that,' he muttered.

'The sheepdog with the bullet in its head.'

'I've never owned a sheepdog.'

I pressed on the accelerator again, and he put his hands

on the dashboard. 'Please,' he said. 'My house is near here. Just let me out.'

I jammed on the brakes and we skidded to a stop. 'I'm getting thirsty again,' I said. 'Is there anything left in those bottles?'

Soapie didn't hesitate. He had the car door open in a flash and he disappeared into the darkness. I had to smile as I reached over to pull the door shut.

The next day, I told Jack about the affair. He said, 'Didn't I tell you Soapie was dull? He won't bother you again, and he can't tell anyone about it or he would be condemning himself. That's the last you'll hear from him.'

I asked Jack what he thought about the dead dog being left at my house. If Soapie wasn't the culprit, then who was?

'A dead dog left on one's portico is a serious thing, but I believe Soapie when he says he wasn't responsible. It's not his modus operandi. Whoever it was had a sadistic streak, and Soapie has too little cunning to be sadistic. I think it has to be read as a message.'

'Who in his right mind would send a message like that?'

'Pull me a pint,' Jack said.

I poured the pint of Guinness and set it in front of him. He let it settle like a connoisseur, and just before lifting it to his mouth, he said, 'The best outcome would be that you never find out.'

13

Maura gave birth to a healthy baby boy weighing seven pounds and five ounces in the county hospital at four in the morning. I had been confined to a stark waiting room for six hours, the longest six hours ever. But when I got to see Maura with the baby in her arms, that was the proudest moment of my life. It wasn't just my love for Maura or for the baby. A boy had been born who would bear the name Cambroe and reside in the big house in Cambroestown. He would be an heir to the name, an heir to a family tradition going back centuries. I had done my duty. If there was one more thing in the world I could have had at that moment, it would be to see my father and mother's faces. When Maura said to hold my son in my arms, I did so and whispered to them both, 'We are back. We beat them.'

The christening took place a fortnight later. The boy was named William Creighton Cambroe in memory of Willie Creighton. I said to Maura that if we ever had a baby girl we could call her Sarah Dawson Cambroe, the scullery maid who was her direct forebear.

'It's ironic,' said Maura, 'that Sarah was a skivvy in the house where I am now mistress.'

I held her in my arms and said, 'She is looking down and

smiling.'

We had a huge party in the Phoenix after the christening ceremony. All my friends were there including Mickey Patton, Jack, Podge and Barry the Book. Mickey predicted Maura would have at least ten more. Jack said the days of the big family were over. Podge said a new generation of republicans was needed who would unite the country and bring about a fairer society. I might have said there was an older generations of republicans who didn't know much about fairness, but I understood at this stage the current IRA would claim to be different. I couldn't however stop myself from suggesting that maybe he should get married and do a bit for the cause he claimed to love so well.

Angel said she would be in heaven if she had children.

Barry the Book was staring into his pint. 'According to our friend Lacan, heaven's boring.'

'Who's Lacan?' said Podge. 'Is he local?'

'Why did he say that?' asked Mickey, taking a few drags of a cigarette before stubbing it out.

'Because nothing ever happens there,' said Barry.

'How does he know?'

'If it did, it wouldn't be heaven.'

'Don't be daft,' said Mickey. 'You read too much, Barry. Everybody wants to go to heaven.'

I could see Barry seemingly talking to the beer as he lifted the glass to his lips. 'I don't see many rushing to get there.'

One night I arrived back from work quite late. Maura was already home minding the baby. As I was climbing the steps of the portico I heard a rustling noise in the bushes to the side of the house. Somebody or something was hiding there. I wished I had a gun, but I would have to investigate weapon or no. In a half-crouched position, I crept my way to where the sound had come from when a figure sprang from the gloom like a startled hare. The apparition, ghostly in the moonlight, dashed through the bushes and over the ditch before disappearing.

I instinctively made to run after him, but almost as quickly realised it would be fruitless. Already he was lost in the darkness and his footsteps were faint. When I examined his hiding place, it was obvious that he'd been there for some time. Half-smoked cigarettes lay scattered in the dim light, as well as what looked like oranges. I picked up one to examine it. Each of the oranges was dried up and wrinkled like a prune with a hole in the skin. The juice had been sucked out through the hole like a vampire might suck blood from a human being. They were like carcasses, and an involuntary shiver ran through me. I searched the area, but there were no other clues that might help me identify him. Could it have been Soapie again? Maybe I hadn't scared him enough.

A few days later, Maura was polishing glasses behind the bar and chatting to Jack when I came in. Our babysitter was at home taking care of little Willie.

'Did you hear the news?' she said.

'What news?'

'The election has been called.'

Jack said, 'I'm surprised the Fling hasn't been canvassing more with an election in the offing.'

'He doesn't have to canvass around here,' said Maura. 'It's Cambroestown that ensures his return every time.'

'He might now,' said Jack. 'Roger Mone is going to give him a tight run for it. For the past couple of elections Fling has just got in on the final count. This time I think he's in trouble.'

Like everyone else in Monaghan I had heard of Roger Mone. He was running under the slogan of, 'Power to Monaghan'. There were parts of the county that still had no electricity, and since Mone was a dairy farmer in need of a milking machine it affected him more than most. He had decided to do something about it and declared himself a candidate for the next election. He was getting a lot of positive publicity.

'What has Fling ever done for the area?' said Maura. 'Maybe people are starting to catch on.'

'There was a time when people voted for him because of his part in the war,' said Jack. 'But that's changing.'

'I don't know,' said Maura. 'It's still his biggest trump card. There's many people around who think he suffered personally for the cause and is therefore deserving of their support.'

Listening to them, I had a vision in my mind of a young guy with a limp roaring and shouting to burn the house to the ground. A limp that I knew he'd had since childhood. What was it Dunwoody said? 'Knowledge is power.'

The Fling held a rally organised in the local community hall. I went to it as a spectator. He had several local councillors from his party on the platform with him. Each of them spoke, and every one of them at some point talked about the Fling's part in the struggle for independence, how he had been wounded fighting for his country. The more I listened, the angrier I got. Then Fling was called on to speak. He stood up and made his way to the microphone, his limp more pronounced than usual.

At first he addressed the audience in a few sentences of Irish, which he said he learned while being detained by the enslavers of our people for daring to declare that Ireland should be a free and sovereign nation. Then he listed all the things he had achieved for Monaghan over the years, and finally he attacked his opponents, particularly Roger Mone.

'He's a jumped-up amateur who has only come into politics for his own ends, and all because he can't find his cows' teats in the dark.'

The joke only evoked laughter from his most loyal supporters. After going on for the best part of an hour, he finished by saying, 'It is right that young people today have moved on from the time of the War of Independence and take their liberty for granted. However, we cannot forget that many brave men died for this same liberty. Many others suffered serious wounds, and have had to live with the consequences of those injuries for the rest of their lives. Roger Mone was not around in those times. I take no credit, and want no praise, when I say that I was. When called upon, I made my stand.'

He eased his weight from his bad leg and leaned against the podium. 'That stand has cost me dearly in terms of what I have been able to do physically ever since. But comrades, I wouldn't alter one iota of my past, and now my right to represent you good people is written on my body. Come out on the fifteenth and give me your number one. Show the world that Monaghan doesn't forget what Ireland had to suffer. Vote for the Republic, vote for Monaghan, vote for the Fling Devlin on election day. And if you can't vote often then vote early. *Go raibh maith agaibh*. Thank you.'

His voice had risen to a huge pitch at the end, and there was a lot of applause. Despite my anger, I had to admire how he could control the crowd. I waited at the back of the hall as many people went up to shake his hand and wish him luck. It took a good half-hour before they were all done. Then he saw me sitting on my own and he approached me with his hand out. 'Ah, my Australian friend, did you check if you are registered to vote?'

'Can I have a word with you in private?'

'Of course, of course,' said the Fling. 'I'm always here to help. Come into the anteroom where it's quiet.'

I followed him to the side room and made sure the door was closed. The Fling noticed and said with a beaming smile, 'This must be very important. All hush-hush like.'

'That's for you to decide.'

Perhaps it was the tone of my voice, but the grin left Fling's face immediately.

'What's up?' he said, less sure of himself.

I sat down on one of the chairs scattered about the room and waited until the Fling held my eye. 'Written proof has come into my possession,' I said, 'that the limp you call a battle wound was in fact caused by the polio you had as a child. You were never shot in the war.'

The blood drained from his face.

'I intend to give this information to Roger Mone, and he can have it copied and distributed as he sees fit.'

Fling flopped down on a chair and stared at the floor. 'You will destroy me,' he said.

He didn't have to dwell on it. Roger Mone would have the real cause of his limp plastered all over the county within days. Along with scuppering his chances in the election, Fling would be the laughing stock of Monaghan and far beyond. His party, who he helped found, wouldn't even want to know him. The rest of his life would be one of ignominy and shame. I let him suffer for a minute. I wanted to savour the moment. He didn't speak, and he reminded me of a child caught with its hand in a sweetie jar. What could he do? What might he say? His eyes darted about like a cornered rat, terrified.

After I thought he had stewed enough, I said, 'If you announce your decision not to stand, I will keep what I know to myself. Nobody need ever know the truth.'

He knew I had him cornered and that there was no way out. He looked at me. 'What is this about?' he said, his voice hoarse, almost a whisper. 'Why do you want to destroy me?'

Again he used those words.

'Destroy you?' I said. 'Do you remember a night long ago when *you* destroyed my family? Do you remember a father and mother in their nightclothes standing in the snow watching their home being burned to the ground? Do you remember a very scared child being carried in his father's arms. Do you remember a crazed guy urging his mates to chase the family out of the country? That crazy guy was you. Whether the Fling Devlin, soon to be ex-TD, has forgotten these things is immaterial. I have never forgotten.'

He just looked at me, his mouth half open not saying anything.

'This is payback time.'

'Jesus!' he said.

Just then someone knocked on the door, and a voice called out that Fling's car was waiting. He stood up, a little unsteady at first. His face was white. For a second I thought he might faint.

'Are you finished in there?' the voice at the door said again.

Still staring at me as if I were a ghost, Fling reversed towards the door, bumping into a chair as he did so. I heard him mumble, 'You don't understand. Times were bad then.'

I rose and went up close to him. 'Stand down and it'll be our secret.' By his eyes, I could tell he knew that I would keep my promise.

He turned about and left the room. I heard him being ushered away, and there was a false brightness to his voice as he greeted someone else.

I sat down again wanting to enjoy this moment, but a caretaker came in and told me he was locking up. I went back to the bar, which was busy now every night, and got stuck in to serving behind the counter. I could relax later and take pleasure in what I had done. But I felt empty. A hollowness in the pit of my gut had replaced the rage. There was no sense of victory, just a void in my being.

When we went to bed I told Maura about it. She held me tight. I said I had pursued this encounter relentlessly like a cause, no less than Podge would see the goal of a united

Ireland as a cause.

Maura hugged me to her. 'I love you so much, Josie,' she said. 'But revenge can never be a cause.'

That night I didn't sleep. It was ironic. For years I couldn't sleep because I had to get revenge, now I couldn't sleep because I had gotten revenge. What did Dunwoody tell me about Socrates? 'Never return an injury.'

I would go back to the Fling and tell him that he could stand for the election if he wanted. His secret would never be revealed by me. The next morning I went to his office. When I enquired about his whereabouts nobody seemed to know, which seemed strange so close to an election. Maybe they just weren't saying. I rang in the afternoon, but he still wasn't available. That night the bar was particularly busy. A local family was holding a christening party in the lounge. Fling would have to wait another day.

Again it was late when we got the bar cleared. Finally only Jack, Maura and myself remained. As I left him to the door we saw that his tyres were flat. On closer inspection it was obvious they had been slashed.

'That bastard Soapie,' said Jack. 'He's attacking me now to get at you. We are going to have to concoct a plan to catch him in the act.'

Maura was cleaning up, and I shouted in to her that I was leaving Jack back to his place.

'Don't be sitting in the car gossiping,' she said. 'I want to get home to Willie.'

Jack and I were getting into my jeep when I saw the discarded orange. I picked it up. It was identical to the ones I found when I disturbed the burglar. A hole in the centre and the innards sucked out. Jack said anyone could have dropped it. Ireland wasn't known for its clean streets.

I left him home. On arriving back at the bar, I didn't have a key to get in so I knocked on the door. Maura didn't answer. I thought she might be cleaning the toilets. Then I heard the side door that was always kept locked bang shut and the sound of running feet. Someone had been inside who shouldn't have been. I rushed around to the side lane and found the door was closed. I kicked it in.

'Maura, where are you?' I shouted.

There was no answer. Tables and chairs had been overturned as if a struggle had taken place. Still calling her name, I ran to the toilets. The ladies – not there. The gents – not there. The kitchen – not there. Then I noticed it: something seeping under the counter like a kind of horrific red snail. I peered across the bar.

Maura lay face down, her head in a blood puddle. A hacksaw had been dropped beside her. I jumped the counter and turned her over, everything red and sticky and wet. Her throat had been slashed. Blood trickled out. A beer stain was visible on her blouse. Her eyes were wide open and glassy. I sank down on my knees and tried to mend her throat by pulling the skin back over the cavity. Then I held her still-warm body in my arms and rocked her to and fro to comfort her.

14

Something awful was happening. It was like steel wool rubbing inside my head. There were voices. 'Josie Cambroe. Josie Cambroe.'

My eyes opened of their own accord. A blinding light hit me. I had to close them again. 'Josie Cambroe,' the voice said. 'Wake up.'

Again I opened my eyes. A figure in a white coat stood over me. A terrible feeling of dread consumed my being. I was in a bed.

'Where are you?' the figure said.

I couldn't answer. No words came out.

'Are you in Belfast, Dublin or Monaghan?'

It was a woman's voice. I tried to answer.

'Dublin.'

'Rest now,' she said. 'We can talk later.'

I was aware of a terrible pain in my back. Maybe if I closed my eyes whatever was happening would go away.

It seemed like minutes later that I opened my eyes and saw two nurses in uniform looking down at me. 'I have a very sore back,' I said to them.

'You got up to go to the toilet and slipped on the floor,'

said one of the nurses.

'When?'

'Two days ago, when you were admitted.'

'Where am I?'

'Monaghan Hospital.'

'Why?'

'There will be a doctor with you in a couple of minutes and he will answer your questions.'

I began to get flashes of memory. Somebody was asking me what city I was in. Maura! She was sick or something, needed my help. Then a man in a white coat . . . a doctor was standing at my bed.

'Mr Cambroe, how do feel?' he asked, drawing over a chair to sit on.

'What's happening to me?'

'What do you remember?'

'About what?'

'About your arrival here.'

'Where am I? My back hurts.'

'You're in Monaghan psychiatric hospital. You fell going to the toilet and hurt your back.'

'Why am I here?'

'You were drinking. Are you an alcoholic?'

'I haven't drank in a long time.'

'You were drinking very recently.'

I closed my eyes and turned my head into the pillow wanting to black out what he was saying. The doctor spoke again.

'You were admitted here two days ago covered in blood after having been picked up from the street. It's clear to me you are an alcoholic and that you have been in what's commonly called a blackout.' He stood up. 'There's a policeman waiting outside the ward. I will tell him you can be interviewed tomorrow morning.'

I didn't dare ask him what the policeman wanted to interview me about.

Even though I was given sleeping tablets I woke during the night. A feeling of doom crept over me. My mind felt groggy. I must have slept again because I woke with a start. Then it flooded into my mind. The blood. Maura on the floor. Dead. The hacksaw. My stomach heaved and I fell out of bed looking for a toilet. When I made it, I threw myself on my knees and retched violently into the toilet bowl. I stayed like this until a male nurse entered the cubicle and asked me if I was all right. With my stomach now empty my head cleared a little. I wanted to die.

We were in a little side ward. Love and Dooley sat opposite me. I wore hospital pyjamas and a dressing gown that had seen better days, not that I cared. I felt shaky and still had a sick feeling in my stomach.

'How do you feel, Mr Cambroe?' asked Dooley.

I just shook my head.

'We will require a written statement from you when you are well enough, but in the meantime, will you tell us in your own words what you know about Maura's death, and how you came to be in hospital?'

I asked for a drink and a nurse brought me some water. I wanted whiskey.

'Where is my son?' I asked the policemen.

Dooley said Jack and his wife were looking after him. Then I mumbled my tale as best I could. I told them about Jack having his tyres slashed, and having to leave him home and coming upon Maura's killer when I returned. 'Have you arrested him?' I asked.

The two cops glanced at each other before Love said, 'We are still making enquiries. When did you start drinking?'

'I don't know. Why would he do such a terrible thing?'

'Who?' asked Love.

'I can't believe Maura's dead,' I said.

'Why did *who* do it?' asked Love again.

I had my head in my hands and was crying. 'Soapie . . . why did he have to kill my lovely Maura?'

'What do you remember?' said Dooley.

'She was dead when I found her,' I said between sobs.

'What happened then?'

'That's all I remember.'

'The remains are in the county morgue,' said Dooley. 'The funeral will take place tomorrow. Is there anything more you can tell us?'

I shook my head.

'Do you think your memory of what happened will come back?' asked Love.

'I don't want to remember.'

'You will report to the barracks to make a written statement on the day you get discharged,' said the sergeant. 'In the meantime, we will keep a guard stationed at the hospital. He won't cause any inconvenience. Just to keep an eye on things.'

'On what things?'

'There's a murderer loose, and we have had at least three victims, all of them connected to you in some way. So we want to make sure you're not the next target.'

'Have you not got Soapie under arrest?'

'We haven't spoken to him,' said Dooley.

'Not yet,' said Love.

'Why not?'

'By all accounts, he has done a runner.'

Angel called to see me in the afternoon. I had been lying half-awake trying not to think. As she entered the ward, she said, 'The bastard searched my bag before he let me in, but he's not as smart as he thinks.'

Angel put her hand down the front of her dress and withdrew a naggin of whiskey.

'This will sort you out,' she said. 'I know what it's like to be where you're at.'

The first slug made me choke. The next couple went down much easier. Angel sat beside the bed and waited on the liquor to take effect, like a dentist waits on the injection to numb the jaw.

With the whiskey in me I felt a little better. My stomach stopped heaving and my hands steadied somewhat.

'I don't know what to say,' said Angel. 'I'm so sorry about Maura. Willie is fine. I went to see him yesterday.' She was obviously stuck for words. 'Do you think Soapie killed Maura?'

'Who else could have?'

'I don't know.'

I finished the last of the whiskey.

'Do you want me to smuggle you in some more?' she said, clearly anxious to help me any way she could.

'Maybe,' I said, not knowing what to do.

'Can I look after Wee Willie while you're in here?'

I couldn't insult her. 'I have to talk to Jack and make arrangements.'

Jack called later. He told me I must have started drinking when I saw Maura and at some point wandered outside the pub. From what he'd heard, I had been found with several empty whiskey bottles beside me in a clump of bushes at the lake.

He sniffed his nose and said, 'I can smell alcohol off you, Josie. You've been drinking again.'

'Who could be so cruel?' I said.

'I don't know,' said Jack.

'Has Fling reappeared?'

'What do you mean reappeared?'

I told Jack that I was trying to get in touch with him before . . . everything.

'Yeah, Fling is around. He's having a big meeting on the eve of the election. It's the day after tomorrow. People think he's going to hold off Mone and get in again.'

'It was Soapie for sure,' I said.

'He's gone missing.'

'Love told me.'

'If he went to England he could change his name and be there for years. There are lots of Irish over there on building sites living and working under false names.'

'Whatever happens,' I said, 'I will hunt him down.'

Jack looked at me but kept quiet.

'Dooley mentioned wee Willie was staying with you,' I said.

'Yeah, we have him. My wife loves children so he will be fine.'

I turned away and pulled the blankets over my head in the hope of closing out the nightmare. Jack got up to leave. 'I'll lock up the bar and keep an eye on things until you get discharged.'

That afternoon I was seen by a psychiatrist. He was long and thin with mad ginger hair that looked dyed. No less eccentric than all the others of his profession that I had encountered. He wore yellow socks which were clearly visible because his trousers only came to his ankles. After giving me the usual little arithmetic tests to see if my brain was functioning normally, he had a slightly different twist to the speech I had heard several times before.

'You are an alcoholic,' he said, 'and you will die an early death if you drink again. Now you might say, "What the heck, don't we all die, so what's the big deal?" The big deal in your case is that you will be a *living* corpse. You will be incarcerated among the walking dead. That's a fate worse than the blessed relief of real death. You know what I am talking about.'

I nodded.

'Korsakoff Syndrome,' he said. 'A permanent wet brain. It's your choice. And don't tell me you won't ever drink again. I have heard those words so often they have become meaningless to me.'

He looked me in the eyes. 'Even in here you have been

drinking. In reality the most I can do for you, the most anyone can do, is wish you good luck.'

There was a sadness in his expression.

By now Angel's cure was wearing off. I needed more to kill the pain of it all. I called a nurse and asked her to get my clothes. Startled, she asked why I wanted them.

'I'm leaving.'

'You're not in a fit condition to leave.'

'Please get me my clothes.'

'You will have to see the doctor and sign yourself out.'

'Get him.'

A few minutes later, a doctor came into the ward. 'If you want to leave, Mr Cambroe, we cannot hold you, but I would strongly advise against it.'

'Get me the form I have to sign,' I said.

My guard had been sitting reading in a side room of the corridor. I was almost past him when he saw me. He rushed out saying, 'Where are you going?'

'Home.'

'You cannot.'

'Why not? Am I under arrest?'

'I will have to ring the station.'

'You do that.'

'Wait here.'

The garda went to locate a telephone. I slipped out a side door, hailed a taxi and told the driver to take me to Cambroestown. He gave me a strange look but said nothing. The pub was locked up and I had to burst in the door. Once inside I grabbed a bottle of whiskey and put it to my mouth.

Someone had put a tarpaulin over the spot were Maura had been murdered. I kept my eyes averted from it.

Soon I felt a little bit more normal. I needed to think. I closed the door that I had pushed in. Nobody would know there was anyone inside if they were looking for me, but there was no reason anyone should. I would stop drinking in the morning and go to Maura's funeral. That was my first priority. In the meantime I would stay here tonight and just have a couple to keep myself right.

I awoke with a start. It was morning. I was lying on one of the lounge seats, an empty whiskey bottle and a half-full bottle of beer lay on the floor. Some of the beer had run out of the bottle and soaked the carpet. I felt awful and found it hard to open my mouth because my tongue and lips were parched dry. What time was it?

I glanced up at the clock behind the bar. It said 3:15. But it couldn't be, or it would still be dark. Then the realisation hit me. Jesus! It was 3:15 in the afternoon. Maura's funeral would be long over. I had to get mobile. I staggered over to the bar. Brandy would go down easier. There was none on the shelf. Whiskey would have to do. I tried pouring some into a glass but it was easier to drink from the bottle. I almost choked on the first swallow and retched it up again. After getting the first drink into me I was able to keep some down. I sat on a bar stool, the cold sweat running from my forehead. I could feel my shirt damp with perspiration. I had to get myself sorted, to think straight. I missed the funeral. Wee Willie was with Jack's wife. I wasn't going back to that hospital. I could go to Dublin for a few days and dry myself out. That's what I would do. I would need money. The bank. I had to get there before it closed.

It wasn't easy getting my fingers to dial the numbers because of the shake in my hand, but by the time the taxi arrived the whiskey was staying down and my condition had improved. I didn't want to get drunk again. Just to keep myself at a level where I could cope.

The taxi man looked at me for a long moment but said nothing. He only asked me where I wanted to go. I had taken an old overcoat that had been lying in the back kitchen and a scarf someone left behind them. The scarf would cover most of my unshaven face and the coat my crumpled clothes. The teller at the bank was going to start commiserating with me, but when I mumbled about having a terrible flu and a taxi waiting for me, she got on with giving me four hundred pounds. I had asked for more, but four hundred was the limit of my overdraft. Back in the taxi, I asked him to take me to Dundalk. For some unknown reason, I told him I was getting a train to Belfast and the ferry from Larne to Stranraer, that I had relatives in England. I just needed time to get my head straight.

15

The bottle of whiskey concealed in my overcoat kept me company on the train. Walking out of Amiens Street station, I saw some winos sitting huddled in a corner of the building trying to stay warm. One of them was drinking from a bottle of aftershave. He was a real alcoholic. I booked into a hostel for a week. It was thirty pounds for the seven nights. That would be enough time to get myself in shape again, even though at that moment I never wanted anything to do with Cambroestown again. I had got my revenge for all those years ago and derived no satisfaction from it. Now they had killed everything I wanted to live for.

After I had checked in I decided to go out on the street and see what was happening. Crowds of people scurried by. Nobody knew me. The anonymity was great. As I passed by one establishment the door opened and the sound of laughter escaped onto the street. I peeked in. It was packed with people of all ages. They looked happy. If I had a pint in my hands and joined in perhaps I could forget my sorrows for a little while.

I entered the pub. The barman gave me a couple of suspicious looks. I would have to shave and tidy up when I went back to my digs. A guy on a bar seat beside me had been arguing with another guy. He turned to me and said, 'Who shot Kennedy?'

'I don't know,' I said.

The guy leaned over and whispered in my ear, 'I will tell you, the CIA, and what's more, there were at least two, maybe three shooters.'

'How do you know that?'

The guy leaned back. 'I have a friend who has a friend who was there when it happened, and he saw the second man fire his gun from behind a grassy ditch, so you can take it to be true. It's from the horse's mouth.'

There was a blonde female sitting a couple of feet away who was finding it hard to keep her head up straight. She hiccupped and slurred, 'The horse's ass.'

I said nothing. The guy shouted at the barman, 'Give my friend here whatever he is having.'

The man was clearly half-drunk. I protested and said, 'I was only having one beer.'

But he insisted. 'A bird never flew on one wing. Did you ever in your life see a bird flying on one wing?'

I shook my head.

'There you are then. That proves it. Give my good pal here a Powers,' he said to the barman.

I swallowed the whiskey in one mouthful. They introduced themselves as Cyril and Cynthia. I couldn't be mean so I bought a round for myself, the blonde, and Cyril. Anyway, this was my first night in Dublin and I had to get settled in before going on the wagon. We drank and talked politics. Cynthia was attractive. If I hadn't been so upset about Maura, I might have fancied her. She was a chain smoker.

Our discussion ranged from the Cold War to what the future held for mankind. Cyril said that TV programmes would all be in Technicolor, the same as films. Cynthia said there would be robots for men's work but no robots for women's work. I felt that the intellectual level of the discussion was very high. I went to the toilet but kept getting lost on my way back. A man with a pipe in his mouth pointed my table out to me.

When I awoke the next morning in my room I washed my face, went down the stairs to a café and had coffee and toast for breakfast. I was on the dry. In a few days I could go home, even though I would find it difficult. To pass the time I went to explore Dublin.

For a while I was fine. But after walking for a few hours, a gradually increasing burning in my gut took hold of me. I was getting the shakes. There was only one cure. I bought two bottles of vodka and went back to my room.

For the next three days I drank and slept and managed on a few occasions to keep down hamburgers and chips. The vodka kept away the need in my belly, but now a different need arrived. It was the ache of loneliness, of not having someone to talk to. I went out onto the street. A priest walked past. I grabbed his arm, but he stuck his hand in his pocket and gave me half a crown before hurrying away. I asked a middle-aged lady for directions as an excuse to chat. She wouldn't look at me, just kept her head down and walked on. At one stage I approached a beggar woman sitting on the footpath. She snarled at me to fuck off.

I was pacing the streets when out of the shadow of a building I heard a voice say, 'Would you like a good time, ducky?'

I couldn't really see her but could smell sweet perfume. I hesitated but only for a second.

'How much?'

'For you, ducky, three pounds for a short time.'

'Ok.'

'First, you give me the money,' she said, still standing in the shadows.

I counted her out three pounds, which she put in her handbag before emerging into the light. She was petite with big breasts, and a doll-like face plastered in makeup. She wore a very short mini skirt, black fishnet stockings, a top that barely covered her bosom, and high heels that clicked on the footpath like caps in a toy gun. She made me go before her up the stairs to my room, and after taking in the room at a glance said, 'Ok, honey, any extras will cost you more.'

'I just want to talk,' I said.

She raised her eyes to the heavens. 'Jesus, how do I get them? I should have been a fucking counsellor.'

She sat down on the bed and crossed her legs. It was impossible to guess her age, maybe thirty would be the height of it.

'It's the same price, honey.'

'I don't mind,' I said.

'Which is it,' she said, in a bored tone while lighting a cigarette, 'the mammy, the wife, or the girlfriend?'

'You don't understand,' I said.

The woman gave a cynical laugh. 'Ok, darling, tell your friend all about it.'

'What's your name?' I asked.

'I can be any name you want me to be.'

'Your real name.'

'Mary.'

I told her everything: about coming from Australia to get revenge for my family being burned out, and how getting my revenge just left me with an empty feeling. I told her about Maura being murdered, and about how I drank a little to cope with that, and about how I couldn't face going home until I got myself sorted out. My son didn't need a drunk as a father. I felt I had nothing to live for. I don't know how long I talked. It didn't seem very long. The woman stood and said, 'That's a sad tale, but time is up.'

She checked she had everything in her handbag. 'I am going to retire,' she said, 'and write a book. It will be a bestseller.'

She didn't believe a word of my story.

'It was mentioned in the papers,' I said.

'I don't read papers.'

I knew that for many Dublin people, Ireland ended at Glasnevin cemetery. She might never have heard of Monaghan. She probably wouldn't know where it was on the map.

Just as she was about to leave she hesitated and looked at me. For a split second I thought I saw a flash of sympathy in her eyes. 'If you want to do it, I won't charge you any extra.'

I shook my head.

She shrugged her shoulders. 'Ok, honey. You will get me at the same spot most evenings.'

She put her handbag under her arm, and I could hear her high heels stomping down the stairs.

I felt worse after she left. She pitied me. I checked my money. It was nearly done. I bought two bottles of Marie Celeste wine. The next couple of days were a blur. I was in a stupor when I heard a banging on the door. The landlord came barging in. He looked around the room. There were empty wine bottles and uneaten chips scattered about the floor. The top blanket was badly stained with red sauce.

'It's time to go,' he said.

'Can I stay one more night.'

'Have you the rent money?'

'I will get it in the bank.'

The man gave a cynical laugh. 'When you get it come back to me. In the meantime gather up whatever luggage you have and leave. I should be charging you for cleaning the room, but I don't suppose you have any money.'

'I will get some.'

'Leave now.'

With nothing to take with me, I found myself standing on the street with no money and nowhere to go. I would rather die than go home the way I was. Although I knew I'd reached my overdraft limit, I went into the nearest bank. I had no personal identification and no account number. They wouldn't even check my name. When I began to argue, a security man escorted me out. I went into another bank. The teller there had the same attitude. Then I spied the girl next to her counting out notes to a customer. I reached over, grabbed some, and was out the door before anyone knew what was happening. I quickly lost myself in the stream of shoppers and then hid down a dark alley until I thought the coast was clear. When I counted my haul it came to only six pounds, not even enough to get a bed for the night.

Four guys were sitting huddled together in a corner of the railway station sharing a bottle of wine. As I approached, one of them said, 'What the fuck do you want?'

'Where could I spend the night?'

'Fuck off,' another one said.

A third guy seemed more friendly. 'What's your name?'

'Mick,' I said, not wanting to reveal my real name. 'I'm from Monaghan.'

'Have you any wine?' asked the first man.

'I have money,' I said.

That got their attention. 'How much?' asked the second guy.

I showed them the notes. 'Enough.'

'We'll look after you,' said one of the men.

And they did. I became an accepted member of the group. They taught me how to live on the streets and where there was a chance of pilfering drinks when the social service money was spent. After a short time the days blurred together into weeks, and the weeks became months. I refused to let myself think of Cambroestown and it got easier as time passed. Someone had mistaken Monaghan for Mayo and I was Mayo Mick to my newfound friends.

It couldn't last. A blackness like a dense dark cloud pressed down on me. It got worse and worse. I became very depressed and couldn't get wee Willie out of my mind. His father was a tramp, a beggar and a thief on the streets of Dublin.

I woke up thinking there was something eating at my leg. My friend Worser and I had been drinking Rotgut on the canal bank and must have fallen into a stupor. I looked down. Squirming black rats were gnawing at my ankle. More were eating the side of Worser's face, with some of them jumping over one another to get at it. There was blood everywhere. For a second I thought I was in the DTs. Then I heard a woman scream for someone to get an ambulance. An old overcoat over my face had saved me. The ambulance came and took us to hospital. I got injections in the outpatients and my leg bandaged. They told me Worser was critical. By the time I had been treated my mind was made up. I would end it all. But first, I wanted to see my son for the last time. I felt relieved, almost happy, once I had made the decision. I knew how I would do it. What would be more symbolic than to drown myself in the lake designed by my ancestors?

16

Father O'Reilly was an elderly priest and very afraid of the fires of hell. He would occasionally meet up with homeless people to encourage them to go to mass on a Sunday. He was also keen on hearing your confession. 'If you die after missing mass on Sunday and haven't received confession,' he would say, 'your soul will suffer eternal torment.' So when I knocked on his door and asked to speak to him, the first thing he said was, 'Do you want to confess your sins, my child?'

'In a kind of way, Father,' I replied.

I told him my story about Maura's death and coming to Dublin to get myself sorted. When I had finished, he looked at me in astonishment, saying, 'I'm half-inclined to believe you. Being a Cavan man, I take an interest in what happens in Monaghan. I know the story of a woman being murdered and a husband going missing.'

'Will you help me get home?' I asked. 'I need money.'

The priest pondered for a minute. 'Can I believe you?'

'I swear it's true, Father. And I will tell everyone you persuaded me to return and gave me the money to do so. You will save many souls, including mine.'

He pondered for a moment and then said, 'Tomorrow

morning, I will take you to the train station and buy you a ticket for Dundalk. When I have you on the train, then I will give you enough money to get from Dundalk to Monaghan.'

He was taking no chances, but I didn't mind. I was content with what I had decided to do. I would have liked to shave my beard off for travelling, but my hands were by now always trembling and I didn't want to be cut and bleeding.

I didn't reveal my plans to my mates. They would wonder for a short time what had become of me but not for long. In their community people often just disappeared. It would be a rare occurrence for anyone to come looking for them.

When he had me on the train the next day, the priest gave me ten shillings which was just enough to get me from Dundalk to Monaghan. He made me promise to repay him the full amount. I said that I would. As I waited for the train to take off, in the far corner of the station I could see some of my companions. Most other days I would be among them.

When I got to Dundalk I spent five shillings on a bottle of wine, and then stood for three hours in the rain thumbing a lift to Monaghan. Eventually, a priest and two nuns gave me a lift all the way.

I must have smelled awful in the car because one of the nuns held a handkerchief over her nose the whole time. I told them I was a patient in St Davnet's mental hospital out on day release. They dropped me in the centre of the town. I purchased another bottle of wine with the reminder of my bus fare and started walking to Cambroestown. By now it was dark and still raining. Cars passed me by. No one was going to stop to give a beggar a lift. An old shed in a field by the roadside seemed a good place to get in out of the rain. I had to force the door a bit. It was a hayshed and full of winter feeding for livestock. With my bottle of wine beside me I made a nest for myself in the fodder.

When I awoke the sun was shining through tiny cracks in the tin roof. I thought I heard commotion outside. There was a little wine left so I finished it off and went to investigate. When I slid back the door I saw several squad cars and a line of cops surrounding the shed. Bottle still in hand, I stood there with my mouth open. Sergeant Love appeared.

'Jesus,' I heard him mutter when he saw me. 'How low can a man fall?'

'What's going on?' I managed to ask.

'You're under arrest.'

'For what?'

'For having us scour the length and breadth of England looking for you, for not taking the bus from Dundalk as you were supposed to, and for keeping us out all night,' said Love.

Father O'Reilly was the only one who knew my plans. He must have squealed to the cops. 'You can't arrest me for that.'

'What about breaking and entering,' he said, pointing at the shed door. 'Put him in the car,' he told two of his colleagues.

'Put on your gloves,' one of them said. 'I've seen cleaner sow pigs.'

The two went to grab me but I tried to fight them off.

'Now we can add being drunk and disorderly and violently resisting arrest,' said Love.

In the car I asked them was there any chance of a drink. 'Wine, or anything at all.'

Love turned to me and said, 'You should be taken around schools to show what alcohol can do to a human being.'

I wasn't listening. Once they let me go I knew what I planned to do. In the station they put me in a cell where I lay down on a raised board in the shape of a bed. After about an hour I was brought to a room where Love and Detective Dooley were waiting. They motioned for me to sit down, but I was too agitated to sit still.

'Is there anything you wish to say in connection with your wife's death?' Love asked me.

I shook my head, and Love came around to where I was sitting. I was trying not to shake. 'Joseph Cambroe,' he said, 'I am charging you with murder in the first degree of your wife, Maureen Cambroe. Anything you wish to say will be taken down and may be used in evidence against you.'

I wasn't sure I was hearing right. 'What are you saying?'

'You have been charged with murdering your wife. Do you have anything to say?'

'No,' was all I could think of. They put me back in the cell. Shortly afterwards a young man in civilian clothes came in. He wrinkled his nose. It must have been the smell. He introduced himself as Simon Platter and said he was a solicitor. He told me he had never represented a murderer before, but the court proceedings about to take place were only a formality. I would be charged with killing Maura, and the police would ask that I be held in custody. He would ask for bail. The magistrate would refuse, but would recommend that I be hospitalised.

'How do you know all this?' I asked.

'It's the way it is,' he said. 'In your condition, any questioning wouldn't be accepted as valid in a court of law, so you must be sobered up first. While in hospital you will still be under guard, so you can't get away like you did before.'

'I don't want to be sober.'

'You have no choice. I will see you shortly in court. You may plead not guilty for now, and your plea can be changed later to guilty if necessary.'

He gathered up his papers and put them in his attaché case. As he was leaving, I mumbled that I wasn't a murderer. He glanced back at me and left. My main concern however was the shakes. I had a horror of the DTs returning.

In the afternoon I was arraigned before a magistrate's court, charged with murdering Maura, and asked how I would plead. I pleaded not guilty. Because of the withdrawals, I hardly cared what I said. The superintendent said the charges were serious, and if I was released on bail I would pose a threat to the public. The judge barely looked at me. 'I order that the accused be held in custody and receive medical attention,' he said.

Half an hour later I was in the same drying-out ward as before. I fought the cops and then the medical staff as best I could, but I was held down by two burly nurses and given an injection. I remembered very little about the next several days. All the time groggy, I would wake and eat a little, be given more tablets and told to relax. Invariably sleep would overcome me.

My senses returned slowly. After a time the shakes had gone but not the desire to get drunk and blot everything out. I was placed on a 'caution card'. When I asked what that meant, a nurse told me I was on suicide watch. But I could afford to wait my chance. It wouldn't last forever. A long spell in prison before the trial awaited me, and there would be plenty of opportunities to end it all.

Even though I was in police custody and being monitored twenty-four hours a day, I had not been found guilty of anything, so I had certain privileges. These included visits by relatives and friends. Jack was first to come and see me. With tears in his eyes he put his arms around me saying, 'What have you done to yourself?'

I just grunted something.

'Jesus, Josie, have you looked in the mirror?'

'What about my son?' I said.

'Willie is just fine. Angel looks after him most of the time. They both stay in the big house. I was finding it a bit tight with another mouth to feed, and she begged us to get keeping him.'

'What about when she's drinking?'

'Angel hasn't touched a drop in ages. She lives for your son. He seems to have given a whole new meaning to her life. She is like a mother to him.'

I was surprised but happy to hear this. After reconciling himself to my condition, Jack filled me in on all the news.

'In Cambroestown,' he said, 'everyone knows everything. It's common knowledge that Soapie didn't kill Maura, and on that basis you are guilty.'

I felt like saying that if everyone knew everything, how come they didn't know who the real murderer was. 'How do they know Soapie didn't do it?' I asked.

'The police tracked Soapie down in England, and brought him home for questioning. It all came out. Soapie told of you abducting him and getting him to confess certain things he had done, which he still admits to. He said that you were about to beat him up, only you stopped the car and he escaped. He said you told him you enjoyed cutting people, which is a piece of evidence they are sure to use in the trial.'

'Why would he run if he didn't do it?'

'When he heard the news about Maura, it never struck him that you might have done it, but he knew that you would be one hundred percent sure that he was guilty, and fear of what you would do to him made him abscond.'

'How are they so sure he didn't do it?'

'Because he made a clean breast of everything, and he has water tight alibis for where he was and everything he did that night. It wasn't him that ripped my tyres. It was the killer's way of getting rid of you while he committed the murder.'

'The Fling,' I said, 'I had stuff on him nobody knows about.'

He was in Dublin at a party meeting that whole day and night,' said Jack. 'By the way, he won the election by the skin of his teeth in case you didn't know.'

'I don't care if he's Prime Minister. He must have killed my Maura. Or had someone do it for him.'

'Well he's not the Taoiseach, but he has been made

minister for agriculture, which gives him a lot of power. You saying you had stuff on him explains why the local paper gave an account of his movements that night in an article. He had fed them with it. He was making sure he was in the clear if you made any accusations. Anyway, I refuse to believe it could be him.'

'Why?'

'Instinct. It's just not Fling's style, bad and all as he is. No matter what pressure he was under. To be murdering women in their homes . . . my God, by cutting their throats.' Jack gave a little shiver.

I lay back in the bed and stared at the ceiling. 'What happens now?'

'You will need the best barrister in the country. The nub of the problem is if you didn't kill Maura, then who did? That's what's going to haunt the trial.'

'I thought the system meant one had to be proven guilty.'

'The cops must have enough circumstantial evidence to make the charges stick. But in truth, the jury are going to be swayed by what I am after saying. If you didn't do it, who did? That's just human nature.'

'What you are really saying is that the real murderer has to be caught or I will be convicted.'

'And that can't happen,' said Jack, 'because the police are not looking for anyone else. Even if you were found not guilty, I don't believe they would look for the real culprit because they're convinced it's you.'

'You don't paint an encouraging scenario,' I said.

Jack looked me in the eyes. 'I would have thought you'd be more worried.'

'I have lost the will to care about anything since Maura died, except that she gets justice, and I have no way of doing that.'

Jack stood up and began pacing the floor. 'So you're not going to fight these charges with all your might then? You intend to escape into jail just as you escaped into a bottle?'

'I don't see the point in anything anymore. I'm powerless.'

Jack stopped pacing, turned to me and said, 'How selfish can you get? You don't mind that your son will think his own father murdered his mother?'

That made me pause. In my muddled state I hadn't considered the consequences for my son if I was found guilty. I thought about it for a minute or two. Finally, I said, 'I will fight this thing on one condition.'

'What's that?'

'That you act as my barrister.'

'No way. I am out of touch, and anyway you need the best.'

'You are the best in this case.'

'How can you say that?'

'Because you have one advantage none of the rest have.'

'What's that?'

'You believe I'm innocent.'

'Who told you that? And anyway, you know my story,' said Jack. 'I'm not up to it.'

'Do you believe I'm guilty?'

'I'm keeping an open mind. When you left me home that night you certainly weren't thinking of murder unless something snapped after you got home, like you hitting the drink. I'm not saying you're guilty . . . not yet anyway.'

'Then it's your duty to defend me.'

The next evening, Angel and little Willie got permission to visit me. For the first couple of minutes I was engrossed in my son. He had grown so much, and I could see Maura's features clearly in him. To have a convicted murderer as a father would be awful. Holding him in my arms I made a silent promise to myself. Come hell or high water I was going to beat this injustice. I felt it deep in my heart's core. At one time the same rage burned in me over my family's forced flight, only this time it was more acute because this was about Maura and Willie. He would have a father to be proud of, and Maura would have justice.

I turned my attention to Angel. She was dressed as flamboyantly as ever in a short black skirt and canary yellow jumper, but her facial expression was totally different.

It was the light in her eyes, like a bulb being switched on every time she looked at my son's face, which happened every five seconds or so, that was most noticeable.

'Show your daddy what you can do,' she said to Willie.

She set him down on his feet, and taking him by the hand she led him half walking, half staggering, across the floor. Then she lifted him and hugged him, saying, 'Oh, you're going to be the best athlete in the whole world.'

Still holding him in her arms, she gave me her attention. 'I know better than anyone how alcohol can dull pain, so I won't criticise your leaving us, but I would suggest you try Alcoholics Anonymous if you want to stay sober. I have a new life since I joined. You can have the same, but it has to be your decision.'

'We'll see,' I said. 'In any event, I am not likely to be exposed to liquor for a long while. In the meantime, I have other stuff to occupy my mind like who murdered Maura.'

Angel didn't respond.

'I want to thank you and tell you how much I appreciate you looking after my son.'

'Thank me!' said Angel hugging Willie tightly to her. 'I love him so much you wouldn't believe it.'

After she left, it struck me she never mentioned Maura or who might have killed her. Why was that? And there had been no comment when I said I had to figure out who had done it. It must be because she thought I was guilty. Angel knew all about blackouts.

A couple of days later, Podge, Mickey Patton and Barry the Book came to see me. On entering the ward, Podge exclaimed, 'Jesus God! We had been warned what to expect but Lord, Josie, what happened to you?'

Mickey and Barry just stood there looking at me.

'I will be fine,' I said. 'I just went into a bit of skid.'

'It was some skid,' said Mickey.

'I will be honest with you,' said Podge. 'I have seen fellas on hunger strike for a month who didn't look as bad as you.'

'I'm getting better,' I said.

'How are you going to beat this rap?' said Podge.

'I will tell the truth.'

'What I would like to know,' said Mickey, 'is can someone be held responsible for something if they didn't know what they were doing?'

I had no answer. It was obvious from the question that Mickey thought I had killed Maura without realising. But I had half hoped, because they were my friends, they wouldn't think I was guilty.

Mickey asked Barry why he hadn't spoken.

'Any man is only as strong as his weakness,' said Barry. 'What's there to say?'

'It would be nice,' said Podge to Barry, 'if just once you said something sensible.'

I was frustrated, even angry. Their obvious disbelief was getting to me. 'Listen,' I said. 'I am not a damn killer. How the hell am I going to win this case if none of *you* even believe me.' I could feel tears threaten to overwhelm me, so I spoke slowly and deliberately. 'I . . . did not kill my sweet, lovely, beautiful wife, Maura. Are you listening to me? I held her in my arms as the blood drained from her body. Do any of you have any idea of what that was like?'

I put my hands over my face trying to shut out the memory. There was a long silence. Then Mickey spoke.

'I'm really sorry, Josie. We should apologise. We are totally out of order. Even if the evidence looks bad that doesn't mean you did it, and we as your friends should recognise that. I promise you we will look under every stone, if that's what it takes, in order to clear your name.'

The other two voiced their agreement, and when I had composed myself I nodded acceptance of their apology.

'I interrupted the murderer that night and I heard him running away. That is one fact beyond dispute,' I said. 'That's our starting point.'

All three promised to do everything in their power to

help. When they were leaving, Mickey hung back. He put his arm around my shoulder and said, 'Have faith, my old friend. The darkest hour is before the dawn. All will be well, believe me.'

17

'Just for argument's sake,' said Jack on his next visit, 'suppose you plead guilty and get out in a relatively short time. What would you think of that?'

'How would I get out so quick if I pled guilty?'

'We would make the argument that you killed Maura in a blackout and had no knowledge of what you were doing, and thus there were mitigating circumstances. We could call lots of witnesses to testify how much you loved her when in your right senses.'

'Would that work?'

'It might work, even though in law being drunk when the crime is committed is not a defence. It may not apply in your case. The hacksaw implies intent. But it's an option for consideration.'

'I wouldn't even consider it. I would still be a convicted killer in my son's eyes, and Maura's murderer would still be loose.'

Jack shook his head in frustration. 'Then the real killer will have to be found.'

'In Australia there are private detectives,' I said.

'There's a firm of private detectives in Dublin, but I've never had any dealings with them. Besides, they are expensive.'

'The pub can be sold.'

Jack got up to leave. 'Before I go, I am taking this case on the grounds that you accept your chances of getting off are negligible.'

'I know I'm innocent, and I want justice for Maura. The bastard is out there somewhere.'

'Yeah, I hope so,' said Jack. He didn't sound totally convinced.

The next time Jack came he said, 'I have some news. But I don't think it's of any use to us and it won't really change anything.'

'Tell me.'

'The private detective guys have discovered that over the years there have been a number of prostitutes murdered with limbs sawn off. The hand in the field belonged to a prostitute. Just maybe whoever killed them was the same person who murdered Maura, and remember he had a hacksaw with him. But it's a long shot.'

'Wait a minute,' I said. 'I haven't been here for years.'

'I have thought of that, but over the years there are always murders. It doesn't have to be the same guy . . . or gal.'

'This must help me.'

'It doesn't. It only convinces me a little bit more that maybe you are not the murderer.'

'Thanks for that,' I said dryly. 'How come the cops are not following this up?'

'It's a long way from the police station in Monaghan to headquarters in Dublin. They have never really coordinated their enquiries, especially for old cases. What happens down here doesn't get much attention in the capital. We're a backwater.'

'What happens now?'

'We wait and see if the PIs can come up with anything else.'

I was discharged from hospital and taken to the barracks. Dooley was already there working the nail-file when I was ushered into the interview room by Love. The detective just gave me a glance when I entered, as if he had just discovered something very interesting about his fingernails. I was seated in front of Love's desk.

'We want to take a statement from you,' said the sergeant. 'Before you begin, is there anything you want to tell us that hasn't been revealed?'

'Nothing that you don't already know.'

Dooley looked up. 'In the long run, full disclosure is always beneficial.'

'I have disclosed everything,' I said.

'Did you have a falling out with Maura?'

'Definitely not.'

'Did you have any involvement whatsoever with the death of any Dublin prostitutes?'

'No.'

'Did you have any involvement whatsoever with the hand that was found in your meadow?'

'No.'

'Are you satisfied that is all you wish to say?'

'Yes.'

There was silence. Then Love said, 'Ok, let's get to the statement. I will type as you dictate so go slowly. My finger work isn't the best. Start with leaving Jack home.'

I recounted everything just as it happened, leaving nothing out. The story ended with me being devastated at seeing Maura's body, and having no recollection of anything after that until I awoke in hospital. When I had finished, Love read it back to me, and when I agreed that he had correctly recorded my words, I signed it.

Love placed the document in a folder. He said, 'Joseph Cambroe, in addition to the other charges against you, I am charging you with the wilful murder of Bridget Faulkner, the owner of a hand found in your field, of a waitress known as Ann Rooney, and of Kitty Reardon, a Dublin prostitute. Anything you say may be used in evidence against you. Do you wish to say anything?'

I was so stunned I just shook my head.

I was taken by police van to Mountjoy Jail. Through a slit in the side of the vehicle I could see a pub sign, and I imagined myself in there relaxing and chatting. Then it hit me that if I was free it wouldn't be like that. I would in all probability be barred from even entering the premises. When I got to the jail, I was examined by a doctor and put in a cell on my own, which I was happy about. It had a bunkbed and a slop bucket. The thick wooden door had a peephole that could be opened and closed from the outside. The brick walls were painted a light blue, and the floor was bare concrete. I lay down on the bed and stared at the ceiling. So much had happened to me since coming to Ireland. I thought about a phrase my mother would say when I got into trouble as a child. 'Now, do you see the spot you got yourself into?'

I had certainly gotten myself into a spot, but just now my concern wasn't about myself anymore. Uncovering the murderer so as not to leave my son with such a legacy, and getting justice for Maura were the only important things left. Lying there, the thought came into my mind: I didn't do it, but somebody did, and that person was perhaps known to me. This was something I hadn't even considered before. Now I just had to figure out who that person was.

A couple of days later Jack called to see me. As my lawyer he had privileges other visitors didn't have. A little room was set aside for us and we had privacy. Jack said being charged with the other murders was a ploy, even if the police thought I was responsible. He couldn't see them having much evidence to connect me to them, but it would build a case. The judge might order those charges dropped. In the jury's mind, however, a pattern would have been established. They were dealing with a serial killer, and Maura was just another victim. He said until we had the book of evidence it was difficult to know how to proceed by way of defence. The book would tell us what witnesses the prosecution would call, and what they would say. Jack told me to settle myself in prison and to build up my strength. When I won the case I needed to come home fit and well. I could tell he didn't have much hope of that outcome.

There was no choice but to try and settle into prison life, and as a way of passing the time I spent many hours in the gym. I didn't mix much with other prisoners. It was noticeable that practically all of them said they were innocent. One screw thought he was being witty when he said that in any hundred people inside the walls there would be more innocent people than any hundred outside. I thought there may have been a grain of truth in the statement but didn't comment.

After some time I built up a friendship with a guy called the Disciple. Doing life for murdering his girlfriend, it was common knowledge that after killing her he had attempted to eat her, plus it was said he never spoke at his trial. Most of the other prisoners wanted nothing to do with him . . . or me. At first I also shunned him, but he grew on me. There was something about his personality in spite of what he was supposed to have done. After all, everyone in the jail believed I was even worse. When they saw us talking I guessed they were saying, "birds of a feather". He had been there for fifteen years and was big into religion. New prisoners were told scary stories about him. His eyes were his most noticeable feature. I had heard people being described as having fiery eyes, but the Disciple's pupils actually looked like there were flames burning in them. I watched people back away from him when he stared at them as if they were afraid of being scorched. He kept them closed much of time, in my imagination to keep the flames from going out.

On one occasion when we got chatting, I ventured to ask if the charges against him were true.

'We loved each other,' he said simply as if that explained everything.

'If you loved her, why kill her? And if the rumours are true, why eat her?'

'What else could be done?'

'I don't understand,' I said.

'Roman Catholics eat the one they love.'

It took me a couple of seconds to realise he was talking about communion. It always struck me that I was in the presence of someone who knew something that nobody else knew.

Over the next couple of months I had visits from Angel and Willie. The child could now walk unaided. Angel said sobriety was the best gift she'd ever received, and she had Willie to thank for it. Mickey Patton, Podge and Barry the Book also came to see me. They agreed with Jack that the other murder charges were just to make my case look more damning and wouldn't stand up in court.

Eventually Jack appeared with the book of evidence. I could tell by his face he was in a foul mood. He asked the warder if we could have more time than usual, which was granted. When we went into the little room that contained only a table and two chairs, he flung the huge sheaf of papers on the table, saying, 'What the hell do you think you're playing at? Are you taking me for a fool?'

Stunned by this attack, I just said, 'No. Tell me what's wrong.'

Jack threw his arms in the air. 'What the fuck's wrong? Everything is fucking wrong.'

I had never seen him so angry. 'Please calm down, Jack.'

'Calm down? You didn't tell me the truth.'

'What truth?'

'It's all there,' said Jack, pointing to the sheaf of papers. 'You were a raving alcoholic in Australia and charged with murdering your wife.'

I sat there shaking my head. I was a fool to think that wouldn't come up.

'Well?' said Jack.

'I didn't murder my wife. What else is in there?'

'You lived under a different name in Australia. You consorted with prostitutes in Dublin. While you were in Dublin you lived under yet another name. On the night Maura was killed, there was no attempt at a break-in. How did the killer get in if it wasn't you? Your fingerprints are on the hacksaw. Is that enough to be going on with?'

I just sat there and said nothing.

'All the people involved will be called as witnesses,' said Jack. 'The prosecution will make mincemeat out of you. You may as well plead guilty now and hope you don't get a whole-life sentence.'

He got up and started pacing the floor. 'Jesus, Josie, what's going on? All the evidence suggests you killed Maura, and now it turns out your Australian wife was also murdered in similar circumstances.'

'That's wrong,' I said. 'It wasn't similar circumstances.'

Jack sat down and said in a very quiet voice, 'Oh, it wasn't similar circumstances.' Then he shouted, 'What the fuck circumstances was it then?'

It was my turn to start walking the floor of the little room. I studied the cracks on the tiles as I paced over and back. There was silence except for the sound of keys jangling every now and then as a jailer walked by in the corridor. There was no hiding place now. Still I didn't speak.

'I'm waiting,' said Jack, tapping each finger of his right

hand in turn on the table.

I took a deep breath. 'Ok,' I said. 'You know how we ended up in Australia.'

'Of course I fucking know.'

'When we finally arrived it was awful for my parents. My father couldn't get a job. My mother worked at all kinds of menial chores. Then Dad started to drink. Sometimes when drunk he would tell me I had to go back to Ireland and restore the family name. He made me promise I would. Then things got even worse. They couldn't care for me and I was taken into a shelter and ended up with a foster family who gave me another name. That is why the mix-up in the names occurred when I first arrived here. My father died a broken old drunk, and my mother, stricken with grief, eventually passed away also.

'I grew up wild and crazy. I drank and fought and ended up in jail. I was out of control. The drunk tanks and padded cells started. In one of those institutions I met Molly. Molly had led a life as bad as my own, so we had a lot in common. We became a couple, and on getting released from the asylum, we moved out to the bush where we wouldn't be confronted with alcohol. The small settlement where we lived had only one pub in it. I worked for a local sheep farmer and Molly made garments of wool for which there was a great demand. We were happy. But it couldn't last. The fire in my belly from my past eventually caused me to start drinking again. Molly tried to help me, but then, inevitably, she went back to drink as well.

'Much of the next period is a blur to me. We were known as the drunken Paddies in the village. Most times they wouldn't serve us in the bar and only gave us alcohol to take with us because we would fight like crazy in the pub. One night during one of these arguments, Molly left the shack and said she was going back to Ireland. I was in no state to pay her any heed. She had said this countless times before. I never saw her again. After maybe a couple of weeks people started asking questions about where she had disappeared to. Police arrived and questioned me, but I could tell them very little. Then after about six months, body parts were found in a small canyon. A ring on one finger established the fact that it was Molly.'

'Wait, wait, wait,' said Jack. 'How can you be so sure you didn't kill her with the state you were in?'

'I didn't,' I said. 'Because of my record, plus the fact that the day she first went missing we had been fighting and screaming at each other around the village, I came under suspicion. One resident said he heard me say I would kill her. I have no memory of any of this, but I know I didn't kill her. I can remember her leaving the house that night. She must have died from natural causes, or fell asleep and was attacked by dingoes. Forensics couldn't decide what happened, and there was no evidence that I had anything to do with her death. So although I had been charged with her murder, the charges were dropped and I was released.'

Jack was staring intently at me.

'I didn't kill her,' I said quietly.

He held my eye for a few seconds. 'Okay, continue.'

'The entire episode was a wake-up call for me. I got sober and vowed I would do what my father wanted. I would keep my promise. I would go home, get revenge on the perpetrators, and restore the family name. Australia was going through a boom at the time. Big bucks could be made in the mines, so for the next ten years I worked and toiled and saved and made a lot of money. Finally, I was ready to return.'

I stopped my pacing and looked at Jack. 'You know the rest.'

He straightened his back, clasped his fingers across his chest and stared at the wall. Neither of us spoke for a few moments.

'You know what the prosecution is going to say. You killed Molly in a drunken spree, and also Maura. Maybe you were in a blackout when it happened, but the similarities are too striking for anyone to believe anything else.'

'I didn't kill either of them.'

'They will call witnesses to give psychological evidence relating to blackouts.'

'I never thought my life in Australia would be investigated.'

'No wonder Love and Dooley are not looking for anyone else,' said Jack almost to himself. 'Have you any idea what this will do for their careers? Two lowly gardaí away in godforsaken Monaghan cracking a case that had the smart Dublin guys beat.'

He asked me about consorting with Dublin prostitutes, and changing my name there as well.

'I only wanted company,' I said. 'And other people put the name Mayo Mick on me because it was as good as any other.'

Jack shook his head. 'I can see the jury's faces when I tell them everything you told me.' He thought for a moment. 'Maybe you could plead diminished responsibility and perhaps get the charge reduced to manslaughter.'

'No way,' I said. 'I didn't do it.'

'With good behaviour you'd be out in perhaps ten years.'

'I *didn't* kill anyone,' I said.

Jack turned his stare from the wall and looked me in the eye. 'Ok, who did then?'

All I could do was shrug my shoulders.

'Shrugging your shoulders won't get you off this rap,' said Jack. 'As I see it, unless you can come up with who killed Maura, you are going to go down, and I mean hard.'

There came a knock on the door. 'Time's up,' said a voice.

Jack put his papers into the briefcase. As he was leaving, he said to me, 'Think about it.'

The next time Jack came to see I had a question for him: why does someone murder another human?

'A myriad of reasons. Why?'

'It's obvious there must be a motive otherwise what would be the point?'

'Of course there's a motive.'

'Okay, name a few.'

'Passion might be the most common one.'

'What does that mean?'

'Love, unrequited or otherwise, betrayal in affairs of the heart, sex in all its many guises. Passion covers a multitude.'

'What else?'

'A threat. The victim is a threat to the murderer in some

way.' He thought some more. 'Revenge. You will understand that one.'

'Go on.'

'The victim has something the assassin wants and can only get it if they are dead. These cases as a rule involve wills and inheritances, but not always. That's mostly it.'

'So whoever killed Maura, one of these things you mentioned was the motive,' I said.

Jack agreed, but then he said, 'I left out one reason for a murder being committed.'

'Oh yeah?'

'Drunkenness, people sometimes do strange things when they are drunk.'

I told him I wouldn't be considering that in my search for a reason.

'Maybe not,' he said, 'but the jury will.'

I lay on the bunk. I paced the floor. I banged my fists off the wall racking my brains for who it might be. My main clue was that Maura let the killer in, so she must have known him . . . or her. I considered everyone, starting with our friends Angel, Mickey, Podge and Barry. I had dropped Jack home so it wasn't him. Then I thought of the local priest. Or the local doctor. She would let both of them in. She would open the door for Love or Dooley, plus she had a load of girlfriends. But it was a man I saw, or at least he looked like a man. She would let Kevin the barman in and maybe Angel's husband if he called for some reason. She would let the Fling in.

I went over every possible person I could think of that

she would admit, but Soapie wasn't among them. I still believed that it had to be either Soapie or the Fling. I didn't think much of Soapie's so-called alibis. There were people in this town who would say anything for the Crowleys. In one scenario Soapie hated me and had gotten the hand somewhere and planted it in my field thinking it would do me harm. But killing Maura didn't make sense. He wouldn't have known about Molly, and could never have guessed I would be held responsible for Maura's death. Unless his hatred was such as to kill her in order to hurt me. But that was going to huge extremes. I had met murderers, and Soapie didn't seem to be the type.

As for the Fling, Maura might have been puzzled at him calling, but she would open the door, and he already had blood on his hands. He often boasted about it. It was kill or be killed, he would argue, glorifying his part in Ireland's fight for independence. He had thought I was about to reveal his secret and blow his chances, but with me out of the way he could stay in the election race. Even if I were to say anything now, who would believe me?

But he wasn't the killer that night. I had heard the guy running away, and that wasn't the Fling. He could have got a henchman to do it. Again it sounded farfetched. I got up from the bunk and walked the floor. *Somebody* killed Maura and it wasn't for money. The other thing people kill for is love. Maura had plenty of admirers: Kevin the barman, Mickey, Podge, and certainly Love all had an interest in her, but it was ridiculous to think any of them would kill her because they couldn't have her. Unless she'd had other admirers or former boyfriends that I wasn't aware of.

Then it stuck me. I had been visualising for the hundredth time all that happened since I had come to Cambroestown. The hand sticking out of the ground. Ringing the police. Love arriving with Fowler his sidekick. Taking them to the field in the rain. Love had assumed there was an entire body buried. Into the barracks to make a statement. Love wouldn't say much. I was sitting in front of him and he was smirking, enjoying giving me a grilling. Dooley was across from him pretending to be cool and working on his finger nails. His hand wasn't that much different than the one in the meadow.

At that stage I jumped off the bunk shouting, 'Jesus, that's it!'

The hand. Every time I saw Dooley he was playing with his hand. He was taunting me without me knowing, but in his twisted mind he was enjoying it. He had killed both the prostitutes and Love had found out about it. Love then made Dooley kill Maura out of revenge for rejecting him. He would turn Dooley in if he didn't do it. It all made sense. Maura would have let Dooley in no problem. I had the motive and the means. I had to tell Jack immediately.

'It's farfetched,' said Jack. 'But let's examine it if only to satisfy you. Dooley killed the prostitute for whatever reason. Love being a policeman discovered this and blackmailed him into murdering Maura. Having killed once, Dooley would have no qualms about doing it again. We also have Love's motive. Unrequited love and revenge.'

'Great, where do we go from here?' I asked.

'Nowhere.' said Jack. 'It just isn't a runner. As I said it's too farfetched, and we have no motive for Dooley killing prostitutes.'

I jumped up out of the chair. 'Christ, we have to do something.'

'All I can think of,' said Jack, 'is to get the private detective to do some homework on Dooley and see if he can come up with anything, and maybe take more of an interest in Love. Not that we will find anything there.'

'The bastards,' said Mickey when I told my friends who I suspected, even though Jack had warned me against it. 'They should be hung up by the balls,' he said, his words dripping with venom.

Podge said it didn't matter as long as I got off. Many times I had heard him pontificate that if you get off a charge – no matter how – you were not guilty. It was a fact that you had not broken the law. Not that he believed smuggling could be counted as breaking the law. He always described himself as a businessman. He bought goods in one part of Ireland and sold them in another. And as for political charges, Ireland's greatest heroes were put on trial. It wasn't about who was guilty or innocent. They were irrelevant concepts, especially to the lawyers and barristers. For them it was all about fees, about who won or lost.

Angel said she was praying night and day and teaching Wee Willie to pray for his dad.

Barry the Book said wearing a clown's outfit didn't make one a clown. Podge tried to contain himself. 'What the hell are you on about?'

'Putting on a policeman's uniform doesn't make a gangster a policeman,' he said.

*

Jack was back with some bad news. Dooley was a homosexual and had a boyfriend in Dublin. 'It's no wonder he needs a comforter,' said Jack, pointing out that the obsession with his hands and nail-file was a way of showing anxiety. 'Homosexual acts are a crime . . . and him a member of the Garda Síochána. That would give anybody anxiety.'

'Why would he have become a garda then?' I asked.

'Probably forced into it, his father was a detective as well.'

Not wanting to let go of my theory, I said maybe it would be easier for a homosexual man to kill a woman.

Jack just shook his head. 'Try and stay in reality, Josie, and let's talk about Love. It turns out that our good sergeant comes from Mayo where he worked in his father's butcher's shop for some time before joining the force. But what's most interesting is his hobby. He is into antique butchery stuff. Old knives, saws, wood blocks, meat hooks, butchers' aprons, steels for sharpening blades and so on.'

'That's it. That's it, we have him,' I said. 'He's the butcher who killed my Maura.'

Jack shook his head. 'Wait, Josie, even if we wanted to use it to accuse Love we couldn't.'

'Tell me why.'

'Because as hobbies go it's not unusual. My barber collects all kinds of antique stuff to do with his trade. Remember Dunwoody and the stuff he collects, old letters and such. Antiques are collectable and will have special interest to some people for various reasons. We can't say in court that Love likes collecting knives and saws and therefore he's the real killer. If they didn't charge me with slander I would be laughed out of court.'

'So nothing can be done about it?'

'Without some shred of evidence, nothing.'

'So what do we do?'

'We let the trial proceed as it will and hope that at some time more evidence comes to light. Remember, as we always say, this is Monaghan, things don't stay hidden.'

'Maybe they do and you just don't hear about them.'

Jack grimaced. 'If Love is our man the last thing we want to do is put him on notice. And in a way, although I don't like to say it, if you're found guilty he might just relax enough to make a blunder somehow. They all do, especially if they have no idea they're suspected. But I warn you Josie, don't build your hopes.'

'Have I any other option?'

'No, Josie, you haven't.'

18

My trial would be in the court where I had been granted the pub licence. The room hadn't changed. Judge Door sat on a raised dais at the back wall with a huge harp above his head. At a slightly lower level in front of him were court officials, and at a lower level again newspaper reporters – a lot of them. While the room was the same as before, the judge wasn't. He would have a huge influence on the rest of my life. As much as I could tell about him – because of his robes and wig – he looked thin and of average height. He had particularly bright eyes that reminded me of a rabbit.

Jack told me about him. Like many of the judiciary in Ireland, he was a strict teetotaller and a devout Roman Catholic. He also said the judge's influence in the case would be critical, because while the jury decides guilt or innocence, in reality the judge's summing up largely determines their decision. Also this judge didn't like people getting off on some obscure point of law.

'Will he be fair?' I wanted to know.

Jack's response was curt. 'Teetotallers don't like drunks.'

The prosecution would be led by Mighty Mo, who I suspected would be happy to win this case after his double disappointment in my affairs. Undoubtedly he would think me guilty as well.

The jury was selected. At the start there were perhaps a hundred people, all with numbers in their hand. An usher drew lots to pick them. Both prosecution and defence could object to any individual and didn't have to give a reason for doing so. The judge would then dismiss the juror as not being suitable. Jack objected to some of those selected and the prosecution objected to others. I couldn't see the reasons why. Perhaps it was just a hunch on the part of both parties. Then I noticed a pattern with Jack's choices. He objected to anyone with a pioneer badge on the lapel of their jacket. The badges denoted non-drinking pioneers in a society blighted by alcohol. Only two females were called. Jack also objected to these. Finally a jury of twelve men was chosen.

The case began. Mighty Mo, with all the power of his considerable presence, briefly outlined the prosecution's case. He would produce evidence of a circumstantial nature that would prove beyond reasonable doubt that I had killed my wife, Maura Creighton, Ann Rooney, Kitty Reardon, and Bridget Faulkner, and that I most likely perpetrated these terrible deeds while in an alcoholic blackout. Evidence would be presented by a distinguished expert in the field of alcoholism, and from Australian lawyers who had investigated my first wife's disappearance.

After the court adjourned I talked to Jack. He said that accusing someone else of being the murderer could not be presented as evidence. It was up to the prosecution to show that the person on trial had committed the offence. But the elephant in the room as far as my defence was concerned centred on that one question; that if I wasn't the murderer, who was? Mighty Mo was sure to play on that.

On the second day of the trial I learned that no expense had been spared by the state. Five people had been flown over from Australia. Before they were called to give evidence, the judge asked if I was being charged with an offence in Australia, and if not, why were these witnesses being summoned.

Mighty Mo said, 'M'lord, in a murder trial it is very seldom the case that the guilty party is caught in the act. As a general rule the court must rely on circumstantial evidence. The testimony of these witnesses will inform the court of a pattern of behaviour by the accused that ultimately will convince the jury of his guilt in murders committed in this jurisdiction.'

Jack said the proposed witnesses should not be heard as they were from another country, and no charges had ever been preferred against me. They were not relevant to the case at hand.

Mighty Mo was on his feet again. 'M'lord, innocent ladies have been brutally butchered. The law is sometimes heavily weighted in favour of the guilty rather than seeing those unfortunate women get justice. I ask that the witnesses be heard.'

'The reason we are all here,' said the judge, 'is to see that justice above all else is served. While I am well known to be disposed towards common sense rather than the letter of the law, that is not to say that the accused should be denied a fair hearing. The court will hear the witnesses' testimony. However, should the court decide the testimony is irrelevant, I will ask the jury to dismiss it from their deliberations.'

This was a blow to our case. It didn't matter if the judge told the jury to disregard what the witnesses said, it would be impossible for them not to be influenced.

The first to be called was the publican in the little town where I lived with Molly all those years ago. It was odd to see him again, and especially here in this gloomy little Irish courtroom compared to the glaring brightness of the Australian sun.

I'd seen his evidence in a statement, but it sounded even more damming when being spoken. He recounted our lifestyle when drinking. The rows, the screaming and threats we made to each other. He had heard me say that I would kill her.

Even worse was the next witness, who said that I'd threatened her life on the night she disappeared. The third witness said I bought knives from him and asked for them to be sharp as I had a lot of cutting to do. That was unfair because everyone had kept sharp knives. They were an essential tool on the farm.

The final two witnesses were a detective and a forensic scientist. Detective Rook was a tanned, good looking guy with a shiny gold wedding ring on his finger. He probably couldn't believe his luck at getting an all-expenses paid trip to Ireland. He said he was convinced that I had murdered Molly in a fit of rage or a blackout, but evidence was lacking for a trial to go ahead.

Jack was on his feet immediately. 'Were there any other suspects?'

'No.'

'As a general rule in murder investigations, how many suspects may there be?'

'Sometimes one. Sometimes many. It depends on the case.'

'So being a suspect doesn't really say anything about one's guilt without other evidence.'

'You could say that.'

'I'm asking if you would say that.'

'Well, yes.'

'Therefore labelling someone a suspect is really just a way of not ruling them out of the enquiry, or on the other hand, it might just be a hunch on the part of someone.'

'Sometimes.'

'I put it to you, Detective Rook, Mr Cambroe being involved in Molly's death was just a hunch on your part, and you had absolutely no other concrete evidence to go on.'

'Many cases are solved by people having a hunch to begin with.'

'But this investigation began and ended with a hunch, is that correct?'

'The case is now closed.'

'Please answer my question.'

'Yes, what you say is correct.'

'No more questions, M'lord.'

By his demeanour at the end of Jack's interrogation, the detective was glad to get out of the witness box. Then it was the turn of the scientist, Dr Rigg. I had seen him giving Jack's questioning of the previous witness his rapt attention. He was a small, scared looking man, and I predicted he wasn't going to say anything controversial.

When Mo asked him to describe his findings to the court, he said that while there were aspects of the post-mortem that suggested Molly's body had been cut in places with a sharp object, he couldn't say conclusively that the object had been a knife.

Again Jack was on the attack. 'You say conclusively, Doctor. Was there *any* indication at all that it might have been a knife?'

'No, M'lord.'

'In that case, you could have worded your statement in the following terms just as correctly. "I cannot say *conclusively* that the injuries on the body had been inflicted by an animal." Isn't that so?'

'Yes, M'lord.'

'Have you much experience of examining bodies found in such circumstances?'

'Yes.'

'Why is that the case?'

'It's dangerous out in the bush. There are many wild animals. People die there all the time.'

'No more questions,' said Jack.

When the witness stepped down, Jack gave a scathing little speech. He accused the state of spending tax payers' money to transport people six thousand miles to say almost nothing of relevance to the case at hand. He suggested that members of the jury go into any house where the spouses are drunk and listen to what's said. He said a man without a sharp knife on that farm would draw more attention than one with it. And as for the police officer and the scientist, it was difficult to discern any reason for them being there as all they said was that they didn't know anything.

The judge agreed and was also critical of the prosecution. He said nothing but hearsay and inconclusive opinion had been produced. He ordered the jury to disregard anything they had heard from the Australian witnesses.

Mo didn't seem in the slightest bit perturbed by the judge's censure. He had achieved his ends. The next morning he called Dr Pringle, an expert on alcoholism. The doctor was very tall with broad shoulders and a heavy black beard. He outlined his extensive credentials in the fields of psychoanalysis and addiction.

Judge Door said, 'I want to make it clear that there will be no psychobabble in my courtroom. Is that understood? It is important that the jury is not subjected to such a sandstorm of conjecture and theoretical constructions, based largely on atheistic considerations, that they cannot see the road in front of them.'

Mo stood and said, 'Yes M'lord.' He began by saying, 'Good Doctor, the state contends that the accused murdered his wife, perhaps both his wives, in an—'

Jack was on his feet, 'Your Honour, I thought we had dealt with this.'

'Indeed we had.' The judge gave Mo a dark look. 'I shall not warn you again, Counsel.'

Mo put his hand to his breast, 'Most humble apologies, M'lord.' He cleared his throat. 'Doctor, it is suggested that the accused killed his wife in an alcoholic blackout. Could you define for us what an alcoholic is, explain an alcoholic blackout, and finally how it affects the sufferer?'

Pringle smiled a wry smile. 'The answer to the first question depends on who you ask. There is no agreed definition of alcoholism.'

The judge intervened. 'Give us a simple answer please.'

'An alcoholic is addicted to alcohol.'

'That's fine,' said the judge. 'Now was that too difficult?'

The doctor seemed about to say something, but thought better of it. 'No, Your Honour.'

'Please continue,' said Mo.

'The first thing to be said about alcohol, is that it is a depressant. In simple terms it makes the drinker depressed. But of course in a majority of cases that's not what seems to happen. The drinker becomes joyful, and maybe sings and dances around and does things he would never do if he were sober. Herein lies the key. Alcohol removes inhibitions.'

Mo stood up. 'Can you explain to the court what inhibitions are?'

'Babies are not born with inhibitions,' said Pringle, but before he could proceed, Judge Door intervened. 'Remember my stricture on psychobabble.'

Door by name and dour by nature, I thought.

The expert gave him a frustrated look. 'I will keep this as simple as possible. When we arrive in this world we have no inhibitions. Children for instance are noted for their cruelty. We have to be civilised. The predominant religion in this country would state we have to form a conscience. Psychoanalysis calls this psychical agency the super-ego. Whatever term is put on it, we are inculcated not to do things that would embarrass or injure either ourselves or others, even though deep down we may want to. These restrictions are called inhibitions. When we drink to excess, the inhibitions are overridden. We can act the clown as much as we want. Maybe the next day, after the inhibitions are reinstated, we may not want to hear about the strange things we got up to.'

The doctor took a drink of water. 'Now, Your Honour, I come to a question where we stand on less solid ground. An alcoholically induced blackout, sometimes medically referred to as Korsakoff Syndrome, we think is caused by a rapid increase in blood alcohol concentration. However, there is much work to be done in this area to get a complete understanding of blackouts.'

Mo said, 'Can you enlighten the court, Dr Pringle, does a person in a blackout know what they are doing? Or can the memory of what they have done be recalled?'

'I will, if I may, take the second question first. Sometimes there is complete memory loss. In other instances there is partial or fragmentary restoration, which can on occasion be facilitated by cueing or reminding the patient of events. Each case is different so there is no one answer. As regards the first question, it would appear, despite many studies in this area and many theories proffered, that no one knows if the drunk is consciously aware of his actions and then later forgets them. I personally would come down heavily on the side of him not being aware of his actions.'

I could see from Mighty Mo's expression that he wasn't happy with the last bit.

'Perhaps,' he said to Pringle, 'you could give us a concrete example of why you think this?'

In the witness box, Pringle stared at his hands resting on

the side of the hexagonal cubicle for a couple of seconds. Then he lifted his head. 'A husband and wife lived in a high-rise apartment block in New York. The husband, who loved his wife dearly, was an alcoholic, but hadn't drank in a long time. It was the couple's wedding anniversary, and they had been out celebrating. All had gone well. They went to bed as normal. In the morning, when the man awoke his wife had gone. When he eventually found her, she refused to speak to him. Finally the story came out. In the middle of the night, for whatever reason, the man had started to drink alcohol from the fridge. He took his wife by the ankles and hung her out through the window forty stories up. In the morning, he had no recollection of what he had done. I don't believe he had been consciously aware of his behaviour. I hope that answers your question.'

'If he loved her,' said Mo, 'why would he do such a dastardly thing?'

Pringle had a habit of caressing the tail-end of his beard. Now he did so again before answering. It struck me how precise he was when giving replies. 'It goes back to what I said about inhibitions, and how they,' the doctor made an inverted comma sign with his fingers, '*sometimes* keep us civilised. He wouldn't have wanted to kill her, and in fact didn't, but because of the alcohol there was no restraining influence on his actions.'

Mo was about to ask another question when the judge began impatiently shuffling papers. The barrister glanced at him, and after a moment's hesitation, said, 'No more questions.'

The judge asked Jack if he wished to cross-examine the

witness. Jack said, 'No, Your Honour.'

I leaned over to Jack and asked why he hadn't questioned the doctor when it was clear that he believed people didn't know what they were doing during blackouts.

'Think about it,' he whispered. 'Pringle was very harmful to our case, and Mo will realise that when he looks again at what the doctor said. For me to question him would do us more harm.'

'How did he harm us?'

'Our case is that you loved Maura, and even in a blackout, inhibitions removed or not, you wouldn't kill her. But Pringle told a story where it might have happened.'

'I thought he was saying the guy had no intention of killing her.'

'If he'd let go he would have had a hard time proving that,' said Jack.

Mo was leafing through some papers. He said, 'If it please the court, I call Soapie Crowley to the stand.'

Soapie didn't meet my eye as he made his way to the box. He placed both hands on the side and stared straight at Mo. It probably wasn't his first time in the courtroom.

Under questioning, he began to describe the night when I picked him up from the pub, how drunk I was, and the threats I made against him. The story grew in the telling, and he finished by saying, 'He told me all about the women he'd killed, how he cut them up, how he only did it when he was drinking. I believe I would be dead by now except that I managed to escape.'

Mo let these words sink into the silence of the court, and then sat down.

The testimony seemed damning for my case, but Jack rose with an air of confidence. 'Why did the accused give you a lift in the car?'

'I don't know.'

'Did you burn down his pub, put sugar in his fuel tank, slash his tyres, and steal materials from his yard?'

Soapie glanced at me. 'I don't know what you're talking about.'

'Please answer yes or no.'

Mo was on his feet. 'M'lord, this witness is not the man on trial.'

The judge said, 'I agree. Defence counsel will limit his questions to the matters at hand.'

Jack said, 'Yes, M'lord. Was Mr Cambroe drunk at the time he picked you up?'

'There were empty whiskey bottles on the floor.'

'I will repeat the question. Are you sure that he was drunk?'

'I thought that he was.'

'Might he have been just trying to scare you, so you would stop harassing him?'

'Maybe.'

'Had he stopped the car when you alighted from it.'

'Yes.'

'Did he try to stop you from getting out?'

'No.'

'How far from your home were you then?'

'A couple of hundred yards.'

'Did he actually lay a finger on you at any point in the journey?'

'Well, no.'

'Mr Crowley, I put it to you that you were the only drunk in the car that night, and your testimony here is utterly unreliable.'

Mo said, 'Objection.'

Jack didn't wait for the judge to respond. 'I withdraw the statement, and I have no further questions.'

Later, he said he hoped he'd put enough doubt in the minds of the jury that Soapie could not be trusted. But he was worried that they would only recall what he'd said earlier, that I only killed people when I was drinking.

19

Every morning I was taken by armoured van from Mountjoy Jail to the trial. I could see out through a slit in the side. There was always a crowd of people waiting outside the courthouse for the session to start, including Mickey Patton, Podge and Angel. Love and Dooley and the junior lawyers were usually smoking and chatting together. On the day the Dublin prostitute took the stand, there was a queue waiting to get in. By the time the judge took his seat, the place was packed.

Miss Jessica Adams was called to the stand by Mighty Mo. I wouldn't have known it was the same woman I had in my room, but I barely recalled much of the event. The thing I remembered most was the smell of her perfume, and even here I thought I could detect the same odour. Her bleached blonde hair was tied in a bun, and she wore a tight-fitting orange jumper that accentuated her prominent breasts, a short yellow skirt and black stockings. As she clicked towards the witness box on shiny stilettos, people in the public gallery craned their necks to get a good look. She took the oath in a strong Dublin accent.

There was a notable silence in the room when Mighty Mo got to his feet. 'I will be very brief with my questioning, Miss

Adams,' he began, but before he could say anything more, the witness responded.

'There's no rush, your worship, I don't start work till evening time.'

At this there was a huge outbreak of laughter in the court, which caused the prostitute to look pleased with herself.

Door wasn't happy. 'If there is any more disturbance I will clear the room.' Then turning to the witness, he said, 'There is no need to address the barrister as "your worship". Is that understood?'

'Yes, your holiness, oh sorry, your . . . Mr Judge I meant to say.'

The judge raised his eyes to the heavens and nodded at Mo to begin his questioning.

'I want to ask you a delicate question, Miss Adams. What do men pay you for?'

She gave him an incredulous look. 'Do you not *know*?'

Again there an outburst of laughter. The judge banged his gavel. 'This is my last warning,' he said. 'Counsel, will you please rephrase your last question.'

'Thank you M'lord,' Mo said. He looked at the witness. 'Men pay you for sex, am I correct?'

'Yes, Mr Lawyer.'

'Do you see anyone in the courtroom who paid you to go to his room?'

The prostitute looked around and pretended a couple of times that she saw someone she knew, before finally pointing to me, saying, 'That man there.'

'Did he have sex with you?' asked Mo.

'No, he did not.'

'But I understand that's why men go with ladies such as yourself.'

Jessica shrugged her shoulders.

'No more questions, M'lord,' said Mo.

He hadn't asked her much, but it was enough. The jury would know that I hired a prostitute, and if I didn't have sex with her, maybe I had something else in mind. Perhaps they thought Jessica was lucky to get away.

Jack cross-questioned her, and she admitted that some men are lonely and just want to talk, and that I must have been one of those types. Then at the end, as if to show how kind she was, she said she offered me sex for no extra charge but I refused. This didn't help my case, and Jack said, 'I have no more questions.'

The judge turned to Jessica. 'Before the witness leaves the stand, in the interests of truth, and I would remind you that you are under oath, perhaps you might explain to the court why you would offer sex to someone if you had already fulfilled your end of the contract by listening to the customer.'

Jessica looked at the judge. 'I have something. I sell it or give it away. I still have it. Where's the harm?'

The look on the judge's face suggested he had just heard a profound truth that never struck him before.

The next day was taken up with Love and Dooley, their investigations and the details of my arrest. I had spent hours trying to think up reasons why one or even the two of them were the murderers. But seeing them here in their element, with all the force of law and order behind them, I knew in my heart it was just desperation. They said I had been hiding out in Dublin under an assumed name. A prostitute had been murdered during my time in the city, and a waitress who had served at my wedding had also been murdered. All had been dismembered.

Jack asked Dooley, 'Why had Maura not been dismembered?'

'This is puzzling,' said the detective. 'One can only assume the killer was just too drunk to know what they were doing. The doctors at the hospital where the accused had been admitted said they had never seen such a high concentration of alcohol in the blood-levels of a patient before.'

'Did you check out the saw? Where it had been bought, its age, or any other details in regard to it?'

Dooley seemed confused by the question. 'There was nothing particular about it,' he said. 'It was relatively new, and could have been bought in any hardware shop at any time.'

I guessed that Jack was hoping the saw might have been an antique, but no such luck. I looked at Love sitting behind the prosecution benches. He hadn't reacted to the question. If anything, his mind seemed elsewhere. Maybe Jack was right. Trying to connect Love and Dooley to the murder was only clouding my thinking.

It was the turn of the defence. The only witnesses Jack could call on were my friends Mickey and Podge and the father of the girl I saved from drowning. All of them attested to their disbelief that I was a murderer. 'It's just not possible,' Mickey said, with such conviction that even I was convinced. I just hoped the jury was listening.

Finally, it was my turn to take the stand.

'You are our last hope,' said Jack.

'What can I do?'

'Tell the truth and pray the jury believes you.'

He took me through everything that happened from the minute I arrived in Cambroestown. The worst bit of it for me was when I told of abducting and threatening Soapie, having to explain that I was only trying to scare him for all the harassment he had done. Jack reminded the jury that Soapie as much as admitted that he was let go.

The next day it was Mighty Mo's turn. When he stood up straight and looked me in the eye, I realised why Jack thought highly of him as an advocate. His gaze was so penetrating, it almost made me think I was guilty.

'Joseph Cambroe, you are an alcoholic are you not?'

I hated being called an alcoholic, and I wondered if Mo knew this. 'When I drink I want more,' I said.

Mo looked around him with a puzzled look on his face. 'Did you hear the learned doctor's description of an alcoholic?'

'Yes.'

'He said an alcoholic is addicted to alcohol. Are you addicted to alcohol?'

'When I drink I want more.'

Rather than agreeing I was an alcoholic, I was hoping the jury would understand and be more sympathetic.

'Is it difficult for you to say you're an alcoholic?' said Mo.

'It is not, but it doesn't say much about alcoholism.'

'We will leave that subject for the minute. On the night

you began drinking again, did you have a row with your wife?'

'No.'

'On the night your first wife went missing, did you have a row with her?'

Jack objected to this question, saying the judge had ruled out any reference to Molly. The judge agreed and told the jury to disregard the question, but Mo just wanted to remind them about her death.

'So you may have had a row with Maura when in a blackout, because that's what a blackout is. A loss of memory.'

'I know I didn't have a row with Maura.'

'How can you know, Mr Cambroe? You were in a *blackout.*'

'I wasn't in a blackout when I found her dead.'

'How did this phantom assailant enter your premises without breaking in?'

'I don't know. Maura must have let him in.'

'It must have been someone she knew then.'

'Yes.'

'Can you think of one person who Maura knew who may have murdered her?'

'No.'

'Can you explain how your fingerprints came to be on the hacksaw?'

'I must have lifted it and thrown it at the wall in a fit of rage.'

'Are you the type of person who is subject to fits of rage?'

'No.'

'Why did you come back to Ireland?'

'I wanted to get even with those who burned out my family.'

'Would you say you carried that anger within you for years about this unfortunate event?'

'Yes.'

'So you *are* the type of person subject to rage.'

'That's different.'

He knew he had me there, so he left it. 'Did you have much money with you when you went to Dublin?'

'No.'

'Yet you paid a prostitute *not* to have sex, but to talk to you, to have a conversation, to discuss matters. To exchange ideas. Is that so?'

'You are being sarcastic,' I said. 'I was lonely.'

'I put it to you that Miss Adams is a very lucky lady to be alive today.'

'I never meant her any harm.'

'You remember meeting her and taking her to your room and subsequent events?'

'Yes, vaguely.'

'So you weren't in a blackout then?'

'No.'

'Perhaps that's the reason Miss Adams is alive today. The rage was under control. No further questions, Your Honour.'

Mo was smart. To the jury I didn't look or act like a murderer who cuts up women. But he was suggesting that when I was in a blackout, I was a different person.

At this stage, he asked the judge if the state could

withdraw all the charges against me except the one relating to Maura. The judge agreed, saying it was a prudent course of action. The evidence to sustain the other charges was negligible.

Afterwards Jack said it made little difference. 'The whole idea of those charges was to build up a case. Even though the police had no evidence, they wouldn't feel they had done anything wrong because they believed I was responsible for all the murders.'

'But Maura wasn't dismembered,' I said.

'You and I know that was because you disturbed the real killer. However, I have been contemplating arguing that there must be two different murderers on the loose. The serial killer in Dublin and the person who murdered Maura, but I am not sure how much of a help that would be. There was no evidence of the serial killer being the same person who murdered Maura. In any event, the prosecution have grounded their case on the fact you were in a blackout when you killed Maura. I am at a loss, and yet all the while there is a niggling in me that I'm missing something.'

'But what?'

'I wish I knew. There's definitely something I haven't grasped.'

20

There were no more witnesses. Mighty Mo would give his closing speech on Monday morning. Jack was almost in a state of despair. All he could do in his summing up was ask the judge to dismiss the charge due to a lack of any real evidence. If I were to be found guilty, he would plead that in a blackout no one knows what they are doing and hope I get a lesser sentence. On Friday evening I got a visit from Jack and Angel. I knew by their faces something bad had happened. There was silence for few moments. Then Jack spoke. 'Willie is in hospital, Josie. He has meningitis and isn't expected to live.'

I couldn't believe the words coming from his mouth. This was on a par with Maura's murder. Panic enveloped me. I felt dizzy. Barely aware of my actions, I fell to my knees and cried out, 'Please Lord, don't let my son die.'

The visit didn't last long. I wasn't conscious of them leaving. When I returned to the cell I got down on my knees again and made a bargain with a God I didn't believe in. I told him if he saved my son, no matter what happened at the trial I would never drink again. I stayed on my knees most of the night pleading and making promises to stay sober for ever if Willie survived. But even as I knelt there I knew I had to show my sincerity to this God . . . if he existed.

Many times over the months I was awaiting trial, Angel had urged me to attend an AA meeting inside prison. I had always refused. There'd been no point before. Now I implored a friendly screw to ask the Disciple if he could swing it so there might be an AA meeting held as soon as possible. I wanted to let God know how earnest I was before it was too late. Mad as he was, the Disciple had connections with the top brass in the jail. They respected his good will towards people. At Sunday lunch I was told there would be an AA meeting that evening.

More than half a dozen people, including Angel, were fitted into the small room. They were mostly ex-prisoners. Everyone seemed cheerful except for Angel, who was clearly distressed about Willie. When the meeting started, people talked about what their drinking was like for them. There wasn't one story or feeling that I couldn't identify with. After a while, the chairman asked me if I wanted to say something. I began to talk. I told them of how I grew up in Australia full of bitterness about how my family had been burned out. The only way I could relieve the hatred in my gut was through alcohol. I explained how vengeance became my goal, and in Ireland I had achieved all my ambitions and more by marrying Maura, the most wonderful woman in the world who bore me a son. Then she was cruelly murdered and taken away from me. Overnight my life lost its meaning. I couldn't cope. So I went back to the only way I knew of killing pain. Once more I crept inside a bottle. But even there, pain and meaningless seeped in. There was no escape from the utter uselessness of my existence, so before I came back from Dublin I decided it should end.

I looked at each person in the room in turn. They were interested in my story but not overawed. They had heard many dramatic tales.

'But before that,' I continued, 'I wanted to see my son one last time. Now here I am. All the hatred and desire for vengeance has been quenched. All I can do is plea-bargain with a God I scarcely believe in, that if he lets my son live, I too will live and make amends as best I can.'

As I spoke, a strange but wonderful thing was happening to me. It was as if my addiction was ebbing away and slowly flowing out of my body. As it faded, an image came to mind of the rising sun coming over the horizon and scattering the darkness with light. I had a feeling that I would never drink again, so powerful that it almost scared me. When I told the others, they said that while such an occurrence was not unheard of, I was very lucky to have had such an experience. They also said that my commitment not to drink could not be dependent on my son being saved. That was not valid. Angel said that Willie had been the cause of her sobriety, but if he died then she must accept that fact. Maura's death had triggered my drunkenness. If my son died, would it cause a repeat episode?

I listened carefully to what they had to say. They couldn't know how I felt. I saw now that my entire life had been controlled and dictated by what had happened when I was a boy. Now I was suddenly set free. If my son died, I would stay free, no matter how much anguish I suffered. I knew that in my innermost being.

*

On Monday morning Mighty Mo stood up to deliver his closing speech. 'M'lord, members of the jury,' he began, 'in some ways this is a reasonably simple case. So I will be brief and to the point. The question is did Joseph Cambroe murder his wife, most likely in an alcoholically induced blackout, or did some other unknown assailant carry out this fiendish act? In all murders there has to be a motive. In this case we know of nobody else who would have a motive to kill the victim.'

I couldn't stop Love and Fling and Soapie from entering my head.

'What was the accused's motive?' Mo continued. 'We heard it from the learned doctor. The civilising inhibitions or conscience, which we all must construct or take on board, can go by the wayside when one is in a blackout. I will not mention other similar crimes the accused had been charged with because they have been dropped.'

At this point the judge intervened. 'Counsel is sailing close to wind. The jury will disregard his last remark. The accused is only charged with the murder of Maura Cambroe, and only evidence in relation to that murder may be referred to.'

'I'm sorry M'lord,' said Mo, not sorry at all. 'The accused's clothes were covered in fibres from the victim's clothes, his fingerprints were all over her, and, *crucially*, on the hacksaw. There was no sign of a break-in. He was a man who by his own admission carried a rage within him. This may be to some extent justified because of his childhood experiences, but that cannot excuse cold-blooded murder.'

Mo stopped and took a drink of water before continuing.

'Members of the jury, when I am involved in murder trials and assessing the innocence or guilt of the accused, I always look for three criteria before making a judgement. In my opinion, if all three are present a guilty verdict is validated. The first one is motive. In this case we have the motive. When one is in a blackout, normal psychological restrictions or inhibitions, as described by Dr Pringle, are overridden. The uncivilised being deep within us breaks through. Mr Cambroe was in a blackout. The second criteria is what I might term resolution. Not everyone can kill another human being. A certain resolution is required. The rage within the accused provided him with the resolution. The third criteria is more nebulous, but of equal importance to the other two. It concerns reason and common sense. The law states that the onus is on the state to prove beyond reasonable doubt that an accused is guilty. However, the law has nothing to say in regard to a jury member using his common sense and reason in this regard. M'lord, members of the jury, I ask you to assess the evidence against the accused, and, using common sense and reason, return a guilty verdict. Thank you, M'lord.'

After hearing Mo's speech I was totally depressed, but when Jack visited me on Monday evening he was jubilant. My son had passed the critical period and was on the mend. A river of relief ran through my body, and I thanked the Lord. My mood was such I hardly cared about the result of the case. If it wasn't for what it would mean for Willie, I wouldn't have minded doing time. Now I really wanted to be found innocent.

We discussed what approach he would take in his closing remarks. Firstly, he said, we had to accept reality. We were unlikely to win, so our best chance was to mitigate the damage. He spoke slowly, thinking aloud. 'I will argue that Mo is wrong to say that when you're in a blackout, inhibitions are overridden. It's not *exactly* what Pringle said. He wasn't absolutely definite about any of it. It was all *may* and *sometimes* and so on. Plus, along with that, lack of inhibition is not a motive to do anything. You won't sing when you are drunk unless you want to do so at an unconscious level, and there is no evidence that you unconsciously wanted to murder Maura. In fact Pringle's evidence has convinced me you are not the killer. If you think about it, you would have wanted to kill Maura when you were sober only you just weren't aware of it. To my mind that is ridiculous.'

'I thought you were already convinced? I said.

'Now I'm totally convinced. However, that doesn't help us much because they think you still did it. But there's the other strange aspect I can mention. If you took a hacksaw with you, why did you not use it? As for the rage, it was towards those who burned you out, not Maura. Unfortunately, our biggest problem is what Mo called common sense and reason, which is just another way of saying: if you didn't do it, then who did?'

Jack considered his options in silence for a minute or two, and then he said, 'I will emphasise all these aspects, and argue as best I can that we have shown in your normal everyday life you are as kind and helpful as any other human being. If they do decide you killed Maura, I can say that's not the real you. I think our best hope is to point out you have given up alcohol for good, and pray you get a low sentence.'

'I will still be a convicted murderer in my son's eyes and Maura's killer will still be free.'

'You may not have killed Maura, but the honest truth is, Josie, you brought much of this on yourself.'

'How have I? Everything has been taken from me.'

'If you had called the police that night instead of hitting the bottle, the real culprit may have been caught.'

I couldn't meet his eye and knew he was right. He rose, gripped my shoulder and told me to get some sleep. In the morning, he would do the best he could.

21

I said goodbye to the Disciple the next morning at breakfast. If convicted, I would be put into a different wing. The Disciple didn't eat much and usually just sat there looking at the table. I told him about Willie's recovery, and he said he knew about Willie. I had learned enough about him to know this was his way of talking. I thanked him for his friendship with me. He just nodded and I turned to leave. Just as I was doing so he grabbed me by the arm in a fierce grip. His eyes were blazing. I tried to break loose from his hold. In a strange unworldly tone, he said, 'See what you will see and remember. Then you will know.'

His demeanour was such that I would have been frightened if I hadn't so much else to worry about. Finally he let me go and went back to staring at the table. It crossed my mind that it was no wonder the other inmates were wary of him.

As usual I was handcuffed to a prison officer in the van. I looked out at the sky from the little window and wondered when I would be free to lie in the long grass of a meadow and watch the clouds go by. Maybe never. I might die in jail. As we approached the courthouse, I watched out for the usual gang gathered to smoke and gossip. There was nobody about. Today was different. There would be a verdict, and everyone was already inside. Empty crisp bags, mineral bottles and other rubbish lay strewn on the ground where they had gathered.

And then I saw it. Amidst the litter. An unpeeled orange with a hole in it, sucked dry like a prune. For a second I didn't know what to think and then, *Oh God. See what you will see and remember.*

I must have let out a gasp because the prison officer automatically checked my handcuffs. From inside the van, I could see the cigarettes were half-smoked, just like the ones I discovered when the intruder was hiding in the bushes. I closed my eyes and covered my face with my hands to try and think. Whoever had sucked the orange lying among the rubbish was the murderer. He would have dismembered Maura if I hadn't come back. He was the same person who slashed Jack's tyres that night. He was somebody I knew, since Maura let him in. My mind was racing like an out of control cinema newsreel. All kinds of past scenes were flashing up. I had to tell Jack.

I was taken into the courtroom and seated in my usual place beside a prison officer. I couldn't stop myself from saying to the prison officer that I knew who did it, even if I didn't really, but I almost felt I did. The screw give me a sympathetic look and told me to stay quiet. Sometimes Jack got a few minutes with me before the judge came out. The courtroom staff filed in. Jack was among them holding a sheaf of papers under his arm. I waved to him frantically that I wanted to speak to him. When he came over it gushed out of me. 'I know who did it, I know who did it.'

Jack had a shocked unbelieving look on his face. 'Slow up,' he said. 'You know who killed Maura?'

'I almost know,' I said. It was starting to strike me that I had clues but still didn't know where they led. They were only clues.

'For God's sake, Josie, I'm about to sum up.'

I told Jack what I'd seen and what it meant. For a moment he could hardly speak, except to mutter, 'Jesus, who is it?'

'It's someone in this building, at this trial, someone in that public gallery,' I said. 'It has to be. They were waiting to get in with everyone else.'

We looked up at the public gallery. It was packed with all kinds of people wanting to hear the verdict. My supporters were all there: Podge, Angel, Mickey, Jack's wife, Barry the Book, and others. Podge was wearing his usual bright tie. He seemed at home in his seat. Very likely he had occupied it before on several occasions. Angel looked very smart in a blue suit. I speculated for a second about who was minding Wee Willie. Mickey had his arms folded, which was a way of disguising the missing limb. Jack's wife, who shunned the limelight at all times, had a black overcoat on. Barry the Book sported his flat tartan cap, and I wondered how he got away with wearing it in court. Even Pringle had come in to hear the verdict. He must have been interested since Korsakoff Syndrome played such a crucial part.

'The Disciple said I would remember,' was all I could say.

'For Christ's sake,' said Jack, clearly frustrated. 'We don't need a crazy lunatic to tell us who was eating the orange. We have to find him and quick otherwise the sentencing will proceed. Go over every person in the gallery and think of the orange.'

I started again with my four friends but didn't waste much time on them. Angela saw me looking at her and gave me a thumbs up. The other three saw her do this and they each gave me a thumbs up. If they only knew what I knew maybe they could help. My gaze went to the next person. It was a middle-aged woman wearing a brown overcoat. What interest had she in the trial? But she wasn't the one. It had to be a man. There was a man next to her, a man with a thin face and I imagined furtive eyes. Could he be the murderer? He put up one of his hands to rub his cheek. A thought entered my head. Something about the thumbs up from the others. My . . . my knees went weak even though I was sitting down. My mouth dried up and I grabbed Jack by the arm. For a second I was hoarse. Then my voice returned.

'How would you peel an orange if you only had one hand?'

'What are you on about? How would I . . . ' He didn't finish the sentence. The blood drained from his face. 'Jesus,' he murmured. 'Mickey.'

'It has to be him,' I said. 'Maura would have let him in no problem, and all the times he smoked in the bar, I never once saw him finish a cigarette. Just like the ones I found in the bushes.'

'Give me a minute,' said Jack, thinking like a lawyer. 'Motive?'

'He was daft about Maura. That's the motive. Jealousy, since she married me.'

Jack shook his head. 'It has to be more than that. And

what about the other murders?'

I could hardly think with everything running through my head. 'I don't know. Maybe he didn't do those ones,' I said.

'He did them. Remember the hand in the field. But why? We have to come up with something or you'll be convicted,' said Jack, his head bobbing furiously. He slapped his forehead several times. 'Oh, Christ. Motive, motive, motive,' he cried almost out loud.

'We know who it is anyway,' I said.

'No good, no good,' said Jack. 'Look up at him. He is clever enough to know we need proof.'

Mickey was regarding our frantic, hushed conversation with some interest, perhaps concern. The tipstaff appeared from the judge's chambers. Soon he would shout, 'All rise,' and the judge would come out. I could tell Jack's mind was racing.

'It was all women that were murdered,' he said. 'It has to have been something to do with sex.'

'But the police said the women hadn't been . . . interfered with. Maybe he's just a madman.'

'No, no, no,' said Jack and then, 'Jesus! That's it. I have it. Oh my God, what will I do?'

Before I could ask him what he had, the tipstaff bellowed for us to get to our feet. Mickey was no madman. I hadn't meant it in a real sense. Judge Door entered the courtroom from behind a curtain like a priest coming out to say mass. He took his seat, barely glanced around the room, and said briskly, 'Is the defence ready to deliver their closing speech?'

Jack hurried over to his place at the table and faced the judge. 'M'lord,' he said. I could detect a quiver in his voice, and he couldn't control the twitch in his head. 'I am about to make an unusual request.'

The judge glowered at him. 'What is the request?'

'I wish to recall a previous witness.'

The glower became a scowl. 'This is a *highly* unusual request, one that I am loath to grant.'

'It's of the utmost importance to my case, M'lord,' said Jack, straining towards the bench in his eagerness.

'Will the counsel please resume his seat,' said the judge. 'This trial has long since gone past the stage of calling witnesses.'

'There have been important developments, M'lord. It is essential for my client that the witness be questioned again.'

I couldn't follow Jack's thinking. Mickey wasn't likely to confess in the witness box.

Judge Door pondered for a moment. 'I will allow counsel to make whatever points you would have put to the proposed witness in your closing speech, and ask the jury to take them into account when reaching a verdict . . . if relevant.'

I watched Jack closely as he tried to make up his mind on what to do or say next. He had his head down staring at the desk. After a few moments, he lifted his chin and looked straight at the judge. He took a deep breath before speaking. 'M'lord, I cannot proceed without calling this witness. If you grant my request, I will name in open court the real killer of Maura Cambroe, Ann Rooney, Bridget Faulkner, Kitty Reardon, and perhaps others.' He pointed in the general direction of the public gallery. 'The murderer is here today sitting on those benches.'

There was uproar. People in the gallery looked at each other and began speaking out loud. The members of the jury stared at the judge, and even Door seemed shocked and unsure of what to do. Mickey sat looking straight ahead. The judge began banging his gavel, but there was no let-up in the noise. Jack used the commotion to have a word in the ear of a reporter who was sitting close by. The reporter listened carefully, nodded, and then slipped out of the courtroom. Next to me the prison officer, who practically never spoke, whispered that in twenty years he had never witnessed such an event. He hoped for my barrister's sake that he knew what he was doing. If Jack was trying to make a fool of the court, not only would his career be over, he would most likely get time.

It took several minutes for order to be restored. The judge continued to bang his gavel until an edgy quiet settled over the room. He asked Mo if he had any objections to Jack's request.

The prosecutor didn't seem to know what attitude to adopt. Half out of his seat, he said, 'This proposal by my learned colleague will have the most serious consequences if he is bluffing.'

Door stopped him. 'Will counsel elaborate on what he means by bluffing?'

I could see the judge was playing for time before figuring out what to do.

Mo stood up. 'My colleague has stated that the real killer, not the accused, is present today in court. Does he suspect, for some unknown reason, that he can get this person to confess in the witness box? That would be quite absurd. My colleague has not practised law for a long time. He is dangerously out of his depth and is making a mockery of proceedings . . . and of you, M'lord. This trial is not an episode of *Perry Mason* on television.'

The judge nodded to Jack for a response.

'I assure the court that I am fully aware of the consequences of my actions, and I would ask M'lord to take into account that I am staking my reputation on these matters, and to accept my bona fides.'

The judge paused to consider this. In the silence, I heard the creak of the door as the reporter crept back in. He walked quietly up to Jack and placed a brown paper bag containing something on the table beside him. Jack's eyes hardly flickered in acknowledgement. The judge had been looking into the middle distance, but he returned his focus to the court and said, 'I will grant your request.'

'I thank you, M'lord,' said Jack. 'Before I call my witness, I must ask the court to grant me one more indulgence.'

'What is it now, Counsel?' said the judge impatiently.

Jack put his hand in the paper bag and took out an orange. Everyone, including the judge, stared at it. Jack held the orange in one hand at arm's length, and with his thumb he attempted to punch a hole in the peel. It was difficult but he eventually managed to make a small hole. It would be easy for Mickey with his thumb strength. Then he set it on the table in front of him. There was absolute silence in the courtroom. Even the judge had a puzzled look on his face. We all waited to hear Jack call his witness. The anticipation was palpable. Only I knew it would be Mickey. My worry was how would Jack get him to confess. We had nothing on him except the way he might peel an orange. Someone coughed away at the back of the courtroom. Jack kept fiddling with papers on his desk. Mo whispered something to a colleague. Finally, Jack called out in a clear voice, 'M'lord, I call Dr Pringle to the stand.'

A gasp of surprise rippled through the courtroom. It included me. What was Jack doing? I hoped he knew. Pringle's face registered shock, but after a slight hesitation he rose and made his way to the witness box. I looked over at Mickey. He sat with his arms folded and his face impassive. He had to know Jack was on to him, and I suspected at least some others, maybe Podge or Barry, may also have associated the orange with Mickey. They were bound to have seen him eating it in that fashion. Maybe those who knew about it were afraid to look at him.

Every head in the room turned to where Dr Pringle was seated. The judge said to Jack, 'I will grant you a certain amount of leeway, but don't push the boat out too far. I want to remind the witness that he is still under oath.'

Jack stood up and paused for a couple of seconds while leafing through the documents of a folder. Others wouldn't notice it, but because I knew him so well I could tell he was shaking with nervousness. Despite the numbers packed tightly together, there wasn't a sound in the courtroom.

When Jack went to speak, the first words didn't come out clearly, and he had to repeat them. 'Dr Pringle,' he said, 'I am looking through the notes of your résumé that were provided by prosecution counsel. It says you are an expert on addiction, substance abuse and the psychology of human compulsion. But I am more interested in another aspect of your research. I see that your PhD thesis had to do with theories regarding human sexuality.'

There were a few intakes of breath and a brief muttering of voices.

Mo leaned forwards and stood up. 'Your Honour, this is preposterous. What has sex . . . if you pardon my language, M'lord, got to do with the case at hand?'

'I can concur with the counsel's concerns,' said the judge looking at Jack.

'M'lord,' said Jack, 'I will demonstrate that Maura's murder, and all the others previously mentioned, were sexually motivated.'

'This theory should have been presented at a much earlier stage in the proceedings,' said Mo. 'The prosecution finds itself in a position of not having had time to study in detail the defence's argument.'

'Is the court going to have to listen to some theoretical gobbledegook on matters pertaining to sex?' said the judge.

'M'lord,' said Jack, 'I say again. The implications throughout this case have been that the murder of Maura Cambroe had nothing to do with what we loosely call sex. I now contend the opposite.'

'Law,' said Mighty Mo, 'is grounded on long-established principles. Who can argue that the court hasn't bent over backwards to give the defence every chance in this regard?'

'M'lord, my learned colleague is correct,' said Jack in a noticeably stronger voice. 'Courtroom law is grounded on procedure and tradition, but surely the cornerstone of justice is common sense and reason.'

I could tell by Mo's face he knew that Jack had won the

argument. Judge Door prided himself on using common sense over strict interpretation of the law.

'You may proceed with your questions,' he said.

'Thank you, M'lord,' Jack said, taking a breath. 'Dr Pringle, could you state briefly the subject of your thesis.'

The doctor caressed the bottom of his beard. 'It explored the ways a human person comes into being as a sexually desiring individual.'

Jack closed the folder and placed his hand upon it. 'If it formed the basis of your entire dissertation, then I take it this is not a straightforward process.'

'No, it is anything but straightforward.'

'Would you tell us in layman's terms something about the process?'

In a clear voice, Pringle said, 'Arguably, this body I inhabit was created for one purpose. That purpose is to replicate itself. Now if that's the reason for my existence, then the instinct to fulfil that purpose will be, to put it mildly, strong. Some animals will fight to the death to achieve this aim . . . and remember we are animals after all.'

Mo stood up. 'The Good Book teaches me that I am here to save my soul, not to make another me.'

Pringle wasn't fazed. 'The Good Book is not my field,' he said. 'Of course there are other instincts such as self-preservation, and the instinct to eat known as the oral instinct. A calf will search for the teat as a baby will search for the nipple. However, humans are different from all other species, as I can explain.'

'It's not necessary to explain,' interjected the judge. 'We all know humans are different to animals. We have an immortal soul.'

The psychologist hesitated and pulled at his beard. 'That may be,' he said in his precise tone, 'but there are other differences. In the animal kingdom, sexual desire has only one aim, which is to produce offspring for a particular species.

'It's not so straightforward when it comes to humans. One's sexual desire is not necessarily geared towards that outcome. This is because although essentially innate, our sexual drive is not particularised at birth. It has to be constructed, and each of us, for whatever reason, constructs it in our own way. So in common terms, "what turns us on" may not have anything to do with procreation. If nothing else, the fact some people's desire for intimacy is geared towards those of their own sex teaches us the truth of such phenomena.'

Mo jumped up as if struck by an electric shock. 'This is outrageous, M'lord. This so-called expert witness is promoting evil practices, which I would remind the court are against, not alone the law of God, but also the laws of our nation. It is foreign to our way of thinking in this, thanks be to the almighty, Christian land. The defence is misusing the indulgence of the court.'

The judge straightened the cape over his shoulders by pulling it down with both hands and directed his gaze towards Jack. 'I caution you, Counsel. Do not test my limits. This is not a forum for promoting agendas associated with atheism. Our long-suffering citizenry have to be protected from paganism and the unholy practices that are now becoming so prevalent. This court will not stand idly by and allow such propaganda to occur. One's soul is not for sale at such a cheap price.'

Jack stood up. 'M'lord, a man is on trial for murder. The guilt or innocence of that man is what's at stake here, not a moral debate on sexuality. If an innocent man were to be found guilty because the court was sensitive to the defence witness's evidence, that stain would occur not alone on this court but also on the legal maxim that every man has the right to an impartial trial in front of a panel of his peers, and furthermore have the opportunity to defend himself by all legal means. No words spoken in this court by my witness will break any law. By his testimony I will prove the defendant innocent as charged, but I will also reveal the real killer of Maura Cambroe. My witness must be heard.'

The judge pursed his lips and paused. The courtroom was silent. Finally he spoke. 'The witness may continue, albeit with the caveat that he is sailing very close to the wind.'

Pringle waited until Door nodded to him before stretching himself up to his full height, like a lecturer in a college theatre.

'All kinds of things can and do happen to each one of us during the maturing process. The personal experiences we encounter explain why we find particular things sexually exciting. You will remember in my earlier testimony, I described how we have to be civilised, and the way inhibitions need to be instilled.

'Many of these less desirable traits are not completely disposed of. They return in a modified form during sexual activity. A simple example is passionate kissing. It has no role whatsoever in procreation. It is in fact a modified form of the oral instinct. "Love-bites" fall into the same category. Who has not heard the phase, "I love you so much I could eat you"? Or one that perhaps has relevance to the present case, "I loved her to bits".

'This is fine. People may say everyone to their own. However, if some unique psychical event happens at a time of sexual efflorescence, then what is known as a fixation can occur. Most of these are harmless, and are in fact the reason why particular zones on the body are eroticised, such as an earlobe or toe sucking.'

The judge shifted uncomfortably in his seat.

Pringle continued. 'That said, although absolutely normal in a real sense, society and the law may take a dim view of other fixations. A simple example is the person who steals ladies underwear from a clothesline.' The phycologist paused. 'And in rare cases, things can go horribly wrong. If a trauma occurs when the victim's sexuality is starting to blossom, then it may have dire consequences. Sexual desire becomes fused to the trauma. I have already alluded to the impervious power of this drive. Satisfaction will be sought in repeating the traumatic experience, sometimes on one's own person, or by means of projection.'

Jack rose. 'Would you rephrase that last sentence, please?'

Pringle thought for minute. 'When sexual impulses are coupled with something traumatic, the individual concerned may seek sexual fulfilment in a similar manner, either on his own person, or by projecting the experience, that is to say, inflicting it on another being.'

'Stop,' shouted Jack. He twirled around to the public gallery and pointed his finger accusingly at Mickey, bellowing, 'Michael Patton, I put it to you that you caused the death of Maura Cambroe. I put it to you that you caused the death of Ann Rooney. I put it to you that you caused the death of Bridget Faulkner.'

Mickey was half out of his seat, shouting, 'No.'

Jack didn't pause. 'I put it to you that you caused the death of Kitty Reardon.'

'No, no,' cried Mickey. Bounding over people and violently shoving past others, he made a mad dash for the door with the empty sleeve of his missing limb hanging loose and flapping like a crow with a broken wing.

22

When the police searched Mickey's home they found a concealed cellar full of human remains. Specialists had to come from Dublin to begin the grim task of discovering who these victims were, and even the number involved. There would be months, if not years of investigations. Mickey broke down into a psychotic state when confronted with his crimes, and was locked away in an institution until a decision could be made regarding a trial. Dr Pringle told Jack and myself that it may not have been a simple case of fixation, although he *had* sexualised the trauma of losing the limb in some manner, it could also have been an instance of what was known in psychology as the true and false self. One self was true and one was false. His true self was psychotic. The one that he adopted when mixing with people was false. 'It could have been the case that Mickey wasn't dismembering his victims, but rather at an unconscious level cutting himself.'

When I asked Pringle about the hand found in the meadow, he said that Mickey must have known it was me who had bought the big house. I was responsible for the loss of his limb. In his psyche, that had become the focal point of his existence and therefore consumed his thoughts. He was reminding me of the event. He wanted me to find the hand.

Jack spoke of the way Maura would tease Mickey about his trips away to Knock – a place of prayer and pilgrimage. He said, 'God, could we have been more wrong?'

Following the trial, Cambroestown was headline news for a couple of days. I kept out of the spotlight and refused all interviews. I decided to return to Australia. I was proud of my Irishness, but in Monaghan, no matter the length of my days I would always be known as Josie the Australian. Anyway, my business here was finished.

The Crowleys gave me a fair price for the land. I kept a couple of acres and the big house in case Willie ever wanted to return. When I put the pub on the market, Val Donaghy bought it saying it was one way of coping with the competition.

I went to Dublin and called to see my former companions. Little had changed except that Worser had bad scars on his face from the rat attack. I gave each of my former friends fifty pounds and a note with the time and place of an AA meeting written on it. I didn't suggest they attend. I donated one hundred pounds to the shelter for the homeless. I also went on a prison visit to say goodbye to the Disciple. I was shocked when I saw him. As usual it was difficult to get any conversation from him, but in between silences he told me he hadn't eaten for a week. 'One needs to purify the body,' he said.

I told him about the oranges and dared to ask him how he knew. He stared at the wall behind me and didn't answer.

As I was getting up to leave, he said, 'All is already known. There is no past and no future.' He turned to me with fire in his eyes. 'Everything is now,' he said and turned away again.

I had a headstone placed on Maura's grave, which was in the Cambroe family burial ground. The inscription read:

The mortal remains of Maura Cambroe (née Creighton) lie here and claim a special place in this cemetery. She propagated the Cambroe/Creighton family tree and thus ensured proud Irish names, even if far from the land of their birth, would not be lost or forgotten.

Maura, I will always love you. Josie.

On the night before my departure, I was given a huge send-off. Jack said it was traditionally known as an American wake, because the one leaving, usually to America, would rarely if ever be in a position to return. However, time and time again people told me to make sure and come back even if only on a visit. Everyone was there. Soapie got drunk and sang Raglan Road. He said it may not be a Monaghan song, but it took a Monaghan man to write it. Jack showed us a letter he received from Mighty Mo congratulating him on winning the case and encouraging him to return to the Bar.

Podge declared, 'That proves I'm right.'

'Right about what?' asked Jack.

'He didn't say congratulations on getting an innocent man off the hook, he said well done on winning the case, which proves my argument that the courts have nothing to do with justice, they are about who wins and who loses. Lawyers and judges, money grubbing charlatans and chancers the lot of them.'

I wanted to know if nothing could be kept a secret in Monaghan, how was it that nobody had caught on to Mickey? Barry said the myth that there were no secrets in Monaghan was propagated by gossip mongers to scare strangers into telling everyone their business. Podge said it was fostered by state controlled undercover agents who wanted to know everything that was going on.

'Were you ever found guilty when you were innocent?' asked Jack.

'In spite of what some people say,' said Barry, 'not everything is possible. Podge was never innocent so that situation couldn't have arisen.'

Sergeant Love called and wished me luck. He said there wouldn't be any issue about what time the bar closed. The Fling made a short but gracious speech.

'*Mo chairde*, my friends,' he began, 'most people in the course of their lives make mistakes. While these mistakes can often have terrible effects on others, sometimes all one can do is recognise them and take responsibility. I also have made mistakes. In speeches throughout my career, I have often referred to my part in the struggle for Irish freedom. I am now publically declaring that not everything I and others were involved in during those times was noble and worthy. In our ignorance, families whose lineage stretched back generations were perceived to be the enemy. How wrong we were. Sometimes, however, in the long run, *right prevails*. The celebration here tonight is a wonderful example of this. *Go raibh míle maith agaibh*. Thank you.'

I was standing beside Podge, Jack, and Barry the Book while the Fling was speaking.

'Jesus,' said Podge, 'he's already campaigning for the next election.'

'How do you know?' said Jack.

'Because he never stops.'

'You're a cynic,' said Jack. 'Anyway, why are you concerned? Have you your eye on the seat?'

'Our day is coming,' said Podge.

'What do you think, Barry?' said Jack.

'As regards the Fling, Podge may be right. Does a sheep change its path?'

'And what about Podge's ambitions for his party?'

Barry said, 'Everyone gets a brief glimpse of the sun eventually.'

Next morning when we were leaving the house on our way to the port, I asked the taxi man to stop at the entrance to the old place. I got out and looked up the avenue for the last time. I thought to myself how beautiful it all still was, and of the memories it held. But I knew now that I had tried to recreate a past, and a past could never be anything except memories.

I turned and got into the taxi again. In the back seat amongst a pile of luggage, Angel hugged Willie in her arms. I thought she looked lovely. She was talking baby talk to him.

'And when we get off the big ship in the far, faraway land, your daddy's going to show us kangaroos that skip about on two legs and keep their little babies all nice and warm in a pouch, and we will see people whose faces aren't white, and we are going take our dinner outside every single day of the year, and we are going to do all sorts of nice things.'

The taxi driver put the car into gear. As we passed through the entrance I could see Maura's fuchsias. She had planted them in clumps where they would be most noticeable. Delicate pink bells were just opening out. An early bumblebee hovered over the catkins like a tiny helicopter. It settled on one for a moment before it took off skimming over the shimmering surface of the lake.

ACKNOWLEDGEMENTS

I want to thank my wife Patricia for her insight and enthusiasm, as well as my son Piaras and his wife Marissa for always being on call in emergencies, especially concerning computers, mobiles, and such devices. Also not forgetting my grandson Fionn for the joy and happiness his presence brings when words are slow to emerge. There are very many others such as Ronan Ward, Margo Burke, Noel, Charlie, Kevin, etc., whose ideas, support and friendship provided the essential scaffolding needed to complete the project. Finally, and most importantly, I want to thank the renowned Dublin author Andrew Hughes. Andrew was my mentor, my tutor, my editor, my proof reader, in truth my everything to do with this publication.

Made in the USA
Middletown, DE
19 November 2021

52950791R00161